STAR TREK®
GENERATIONS™

A Novel by John Vornholt
Based on STAR TREK GENERATIONS
Story by Rick Berman & Ronald D. Moore & Brannon Braga
Screenplay by Ronald D. Moore & Brannon Braga

D0011100

A MINSTREL® BOOK

PUBLISHED BY POCKET BOOKS

New York   London   Toronto   Sydney   Tokyo   Singapore

A MINSTREL PAPERBACK *Original*

A Minstrel Book published by
POCKET BOOKS, a division of Simon & Schuster Inc.
1230 Avenue of the Americas, New York, NY 10020

This book is published by Pocket Books, a division of
Simon & Schuster Inc., under exclusive license from
Paramount Pictures.

ISBN: 0-671-51901-8

First Ministrel Books printing December 1994

10 9 8 7 6 5 4 3

A MINSTREL BOOK and colophon are registered trademarks
of Simon & Schuster Inc.

Printed in the U.S.A.

"We have to go back to a planet called Veridian Three—to stop a man from destroying a star! There are millions of lives at stake!"

Kirk looked at Picard as if he were seeing him for the first time.

"Captain of the *Enterprise,* huh?"

"That's right. The *Enterprise-D.*"

Kirk looked bitter for a moment. "Don't ever retire! Don't let them promote you to some desk job. You stay on the bridge of that ship, because while you're there, you can make a difference."

"Come with me," said Picard. "You don't have to be on the bridge of a starship to make a difference. Help me stop Soran. Make a difference right now."

Kirk grinned. "How can I argue with the captain of the *Enterprise?* What's the name of that planet? Veridian Three?"

Picard nodded. "That's right."

"I take it the odds are against us. The situation is grim?"

"You could say that," answered Picard.

Kirk rubbed his chin. "Of course, if Spock were here, he'd say I was being an irrational, illogical human for wanting to go on a mission like that."

He slapped Picard on the back. "But it sounds like fun!"

Star Trek: The Next Generation

Starfleet Academy

#1 Worf's First Adventure
#2 Line of Fire
#3 Survival
#4 Capture the Flag
#5 Atlantis Station

Star Trek: Deep Space Nine

#1 The Star Ghost
#2 Stowaways
#3 Prisoners of Peace
#4 The Pet

Star Trek movie tie-in

Star Trek Generations

Available from MINSTREL Books

STAR TREK®
GENERATIONS™

STARFLEET TIMELINE

2264

The launch of Captain James T. Kirk's five-year mission, _U.S.S. Enterprise,_ NCC-1701.

2292

Alliance between the Klingon Empire and the Romulan Star Empire collapses.

2293

Colonel Worf, grandfather of Worf Rozhenko, defends Captain Kirk and Doctor McCoy at their trial for the murder of Klingon chancellor Gorkon.

Khitomer Peace Conference, Klingon Empire/Federation (_Star Trek VI_).

2323

Jean-Luc Picard enters Starfleet Academy's standard four-year program.

2328

The Cardassian Empire annexes the Bajoran homeworld.

2341

Data enters Starfleet Academy.

2342

Beverly Crusher (née Howard) enters Starfleet Academy Medical School, an eight-year program.

2346

Romulan massacre of Klingon outpost on Khitomer.

2351

In orbit around Bajor, the Cardassians construct a space station that they will later abandon.

2353

William T. Riker and Geordi La Forge enter Starfleet Academy.

2354

Deanna Troi enters Starfleet Academy.

2356

Tasha Yar enters Starfleet Academy.

2357

Worf Rozhenko enters Starfleet Academy.

2363

Captain Jean-Luc Picard assumes command of U.S.S. Enterprise, NCC-1701-D.

2367

Wesley Crusher enters Starfleet Academy.
An uneasy truce is signed between the Cardassians and the Federation.
Borg attack at Wolf 359; First Officer Lieutenant Commander Benjamin Sisko and his son, Jake, are among the survivors.
U.S.S. Enterprise-D defeats the Borg vessel in orbit around Earth.

2369

Commander Benjamin Sisko assumes command of Deep Space Nine in orbit over Bajor.

Source: Star Trek® Chronology / Michael Okuda and Denise Okuda

CHAPTER 1

It was all shimmering colors, like a warped rainbow, as James Tiberius Kirk parachuted out of orbit. First, the black airlessness of space gave way to a searing reentry, with sparks shooting off his bodysuit and harness. Then the atmosphere thickened and became a radiant blue—just seconds before Kirk was rocked by a sonic boom.

The captain yelled with delight, but the boom had temporarily deafened him. He couldn't even hear himself! He peered through his faceplate and howled with laughter when he saw his charred suit. It was still smoldering in the rushing wind.

After several stomach-churning flips, Kirk chuckled and tried the chute. He was actually surprised when it opened, given the state of his suit. Within seconds the parachute stabilized his fall, and he grabbed the controls, firing up the tiny thrusters on his back and boots.

He was right on course! Kirk swerved toward the shimmering wheat field, which looked like one vast ocean of gold. He searched for the target and finally gave up, searching instead for the barn or other familiar landmarks. There wasn't time to think, and he worked the controls feverishly. Darn, if he were twenty-five years old, he could make a better orbital jump. . . .

But this wasn't bad for an old man!

The ground seemed to rush toward him, and he stuck his legs out at the last moment. When he hit, the chute dragged him, and he had to run to keep from falling. Every joint in his body ached from the impact. Of course, he told himself, they had ached *before* he took the jump.

Kirk always figured that one more crazy stunt, one more brush with death, would make him feel younger. It never worked that way. It only made him feel older.

But he still felt lucky!

Strong hands suddenly gripped him and kept him from falling. With a grateful sigh he gazed into the concerned faces of Scotty and Chekov, the Scotsman and Russian from his old crew. They were huffing and puffing more than he was.

"Right on target!" he said with a grin. "I jump out over the Arabian Peninsula, and I end up here, on the dime!"

Chekov pointed to the field behind them. "Actually, Keptin, your precise target area was thirty-five meters that way."

"Thanks for pointing that out." The captain scowled. He started to pull off his chute, and a sharp pain stabbed him in the back.

Scotty shook his head like an old mother hen. "I've warned ye about that back of yours. Ye should have a doctor take a look at it."

Kirk waved him off and tried not to grimace in pain. "Tomorrow I want to make a trielliptical jump. That's where you jump out over Northern China, and make three complete orbits before you start reentry."

Chekov cleared his throat. "Keptin, perhaps you have forgotten that tomorrow is the christening ceremony for the new *Enterprise.*"

Kirk frowned. He hadn't forgotten. "I'm not going." He turned to his old engineer. "Scotty, help me with this chute."

"What do you mean, you're not going?" asked Scotty with alarm. "We promised."

Kirk shook his head. "When I retired, I swore I'd never set foot on a starship again, and I meant it."

Chekov smiled. For a moment he looked as boyish as he had thirty years ago. "For old time's sake?"

Captain Kirk stood in the observation lounge at spacedock, which was part of an immense orbital shipyard. He was surrounded by dignitaries and functionaries from all over the Federation. He had never been impressed much by politicians and ambassadors when he was on active duty, and he still wasn't.

There was a hush as a bottle of champagne streaked through space toward the gleaming silver hull of the *Enterprise.* The bottle erupted against the cold tritanium, and shards of glass spread over the ship.

Kirk's eyes were drawn toward the lettering on the hull: U.S.S. ENTERPRISE NCC-1701-B.

He heard Scotty chuckling with pleasure behind him. The old engineer wasn't happy unless there was a ship flying around somewhere with those letters on it. ENTERPRISE. No different, really, than any other Excelsior-class starship. Why all the dignitaries, journalists, and fuss? Why did he even have to be here?

They took a special shuttle from the spacedock to a shuttle bay on the *Enterprise,* where more observers and reporters awaited their arrival.

Everyone was applauding now, and camera lights snapped on, blinding him. The journalists crushed around him with questions. After all, he had been the captain of the *Enterprise* 1701 and the *Enterprise*-1701-A. How did it feel to travel on the new ship with a—ahem—younger captain at the helm? He smiled politely but forged his way toward the turbolifts, certain that his mother hens, Scotty and Chekov, would be rushing after him.

The reporters even followed them into the turbolift, peppering them with questions and punching their padds. He counted the seconds until they reached their destination, the bridge of the *Enterprise*. The reporters tried to pursue him there, but they were headed off by Captain John Harriman.

"There will be plenty of time for questions later," Harriman told them sternly.

John Harriman looked and acted like a captain, thought Kirk. But what kind of captain would he really be when lives were at stake? Kirk looked around at the blinking consoles and the sleek command chair. He had to admit that it felt good to be on the bridge of a starship again. That's why he avoided it.

Captain Harriman turned to Kirk, Scotty, and Chekov. "Welcome aboard. I just want you to know how excited we all are to have a group of living legends with us on our maiden voyage." He beamed proudly. "I remember reading about your missions when I was in grade school."

The older officers winced at the reminder of their advanced age, and Harriman looked embarrassed for a moment. Kirk finally soothed it over with a smile.

"May we have a look around?" he asked.

Chekov suddenly grabbed his arm. "Excuse me, Keptin," he said. "I'd like you to meet the helmsman of the *Enterprise*-B, Ensign Demora Sulu."

Kirk came face to face with a young Asian woman, and his smile was genuine.

"Captain James Kirk," said Chekov.

Ensign Sulu nodded politely. "It's a pleasure to meet you, sir. My father's told me some . . . interesting stories about you."

Kirk blinked at her in amazement. "Your father! Hikaru Sulu is your father?"

"Yes, sir."

Chekov chuckled. "You met her once before, but she was a lot younger."

Kirk stammered, "Yes, well, congratulations, Ensign. It wouldn't be the *Enterprise* without a Sulu at the helm."

"Thank you, sir." She turned to Chekov and said, "Let me show you the new inertial guidance system."

Kirk watched them move off, and he felt Scotty's comfortable presence beside him.

The engineer beamed. "A fine ship, if you ask me."

Kirk shook his head. "You know, Scotty, it amazes me. When did Sulu find the time for a family?"

Scotty shrugged. "It's like ye always said—if something's important enough, ye make the time." He gave Kirk a quizzical look. "Is that why you've been running around the galaxy like an eighteen-year-old? Finding retirement a wee bit lonely, are we?"

"I'm glad you're an engineer and not a psychiatrist," Kirk grumbled.

Captain Harriman began to wave his arms. "Excuse me, everyone. If you'll take your seats, we'll begin our maiden voyage."

Kirk sighed and scrambled to find a seat. They were getting under way, which was fine with him. Now everyone would be watching Harriman and not him. The tall captain strode to the command chair.

"Prepare to leave spacedock," Harriman ordered. "Aft thrusters ahead one quarter, port and starboard at station keeping."

Suddenly he turned to Kirk and said, "Captain Kirk, I'd be honored if you would give the order to get under way."

Kirk tried not to groan. "No. No, thank you."

But everyone was looking at him expectantly. This was part of their fantasy, to have the old captain launch the new ship. So he gave in.

"Take us out!" he growled.

The applause was embarrassing, but he hoped the worst was over. When he sat down, he found Scotty and Chekov smirking at him.

"Very good, sir," said Chekov.

Scotty nodded. "Brought a tear to me eye."

Kirk tried hard not to look at the viewscreen, but he couldn't resist. The view shifted between the shrinking spacedock and the vast starfield beyond. Majestic space. *It's a lot like the ocean,* thought Kirk. *You could stare at it every day of your life and not fathom its secrets.*

They were still hounded by journalists, but fewer of them had been allowed on the bridge. In due time Harriman again raised his arms to quiet the discussion.

"Ladies and gentlemen," he announced, "we've just cleared the asteroid belt. Our course will take us out beyond Pluto and then back to spacedock. Just a quick turn around the block."

There were polite chuckles, but they were interrupted by a communication beep. The communications officer responded to the call.

"Captain Harriman," he reported, "we're picking up a distress call."

"On speakers."

When the crackling stopped, they heard a panicked voice. "This is the transport ship *Lakul*. We're caught in some kind of energy distortion. We can't break free!"

The man's voice was choked by static. ". . . need immediate help . . . it's tearing us. . . ."

A silence followed, and the science officer reported, "The *Lakul* is one of two ships transporting El-Aurian refugees to Earth."

Kirk watched Harriman, to see what he would do.

"Ensign Sulu, can you locate them?" asked the young captain.

She nodded. "The ships are bearing at three-one-zero mark two-one-five. Distance—three light-years."

"Signal the closest starship," ordered Harriman. "We're in no condition to mount a rescue. We don't even have a full crew aboard."

The navigator shook his head. "We're the only one in range, sir."

Kirk was fidgeting in his chair, itching to give the command to intercept. But like everyone else, Captain Kirk took a deep breath and waited to see what would happen.

CHAPTER

Captain Harriman stiffened his shoulders. "Then I guess it's up to us to answer this distress call. Helm, lay in an intercept course and engage at maximum warp."

"Aye, sir," Demora Sulu answered crisply.

Kirk relaxed somewhat as the familiar sensation of warp drive took over. When they came out of warp drive, a bizarre object filled the viewscreen. Kirk bolted upright in his chair, along with everybody else.

"What is *that?*" muttered Chekov.

Stretching across the starscape was a writhing ribbon of energy. Crackling tendrils reached out and entrapped two helpless transport ships. The ships bounced around like toys, and raw energy shimmered along their hulls.

Ensign Sulu reported, "Their hulls are starting to buckle under the stress. They won't survive much longer."

The *Enterprise* suddenly shuddered, and the people who were standing scurried for seats.

"We're encountering severe gravimetric distortions from the energy ribbon," said the navigator.

"We'll have to keep our distance," replied Harriman, obviously unsure what to do next.

Kirk didn't mean to, but he blurted out, "Tractor beam."

Harriman sighed. "It won't be installed until Tuesday. Ensign Sulu, try generating a subspace field around the ships. That might break them free."

The helmsman shook her head. "There's too much quantum interference, Captain."

"What about . . . venting plasma from the warp nacelles?"

Kirk shook his head, but he could see the journalists glancing at him for reassurance. He gave them a pained smile.

"Releasing drive plasma," said Ensign Sulu, her eyes glued to her panel. "Sir! The starboard vessel's hull is collapsing!"

Kirk and the others watched helplessly as a fiery tendril of energy wrapped around the transport. In a blazing explosion it disappeared. People gasped in shock.

"How many people were on that ship?" asked Chekov.

"Two hundred sixty-five," answered Demora Sulu.

Captain Harriman remained calm, but he looked at a loss. "Captain Kirk, I would appreciate any suggestions you might have."

Kirk shot out of his chair and was beside Harriman in an instant. "Move us within transporter range and beam those people to the *Enterprise.*"

"What about the gravimetric distortions?" asked Harriman. "They'll tear us apart."

Mindful of the reporters on the bridge, Kirk whispered, "Risk is part of the game if you want to sit in the captain's chair."

Hariman stuck out his jaw. "Helm, move within transporter range. Lieutenant, beam them directly to sickbay."

Chekov and Scotty were now flanking the two captains. "How big is your medical staff?" asked Chekov.

Harriman gulped. "The medical staff doesn't arrive until Tuesday."

Chekov turned to two journalists. "You and you— you've just become nurses. Let's go." Chekov led his new charges to the turbolift.

"We're within range," said the lieutenant at the transporter station. "I'm having trouble locking on to them, sir. They appear to be in some sort of . . . temporal flux."

Sulu reported, "Main engineering reports fluctuations in the warp plasma relays."

"Bypass the relays and go to auxiliary systems," snapped Scotty. "Lad, do you need some help on that transporter?"

The lieutenant nodded, and Scotty rushed to the transporter console. After a moment he growled, "Their life signs are phasing in and out of our spacetime continuum!"

"Phasing where?" asked Kirk.

Scotty took over the console, and his skilled fingers plied the controls. There was no time for talking.

"Sir!" said the navigator. "Their hull is collapsing!"

The proof of that was right in front of their eyes on the viewscreen. The remaining transport was utterly destroyed by an energy tendril.

Scotty let out a breath. "I got forty-seven of them." He shook his head. "Out of one hundred fifty."

The *Enterprise*-B rocked again, almost knocking them off their feet.

Captain Kirk barked, "Report!"

"We're caught in a gravimetric field," said Ensign Sulu. "One of the tendrils—"

Now Harriman barked, "All engines, full reverse!"

Sickbay on the *Enterprise*-B looked like the aftermath of a war. Wounded, dazed people were everywhere. *It's like they've been jerked out of their dreams,* thought Chekov. He and his emergency nurses lifted the unconscious ones onto examination tables. They let the other El-Aurians wander around, mumbling to themselves, until the makeshift staff could get to them.

"The colors are touching me!" screamed one survivor.

"I'm caught in the glass. . . . Help me!" yelled another.

If the El-Aurians acted too disoriented, Chekov and his assistants calmed them with hyposprays. In the first few minutes they used a lot of hyposprays.

It didn't help that the ship was being flung back and forth, rocked by terrific forces. Chekov wasn't sure that any of them would get out of this alive. But Captain Kirk was on the bridge, and that was as much as anyone could hope for in a situation like this.

"What's the matter with them?" asked one of the journalists.

Chekov gazed down at his tricorder to see if it offered any explanation. "Only minor injuries so far, but it looks as if they're all suffering from some kind of neural shock."

"El-Aurians?" asked the other journalist. "Are these the people they call Listeners?"

Before Chekov could tell him he was right, one of the survivors bolted upright on the table and grabbed the man's jacket. He was a strong man, wild-eyed, and blood was oozing from a cut on his head. The reporter shrunk back.

"Why?" screamed the wild man. "I have to go back! You don't understand. *Let me go!"*

The journalist stammered, "Y-You'll be all right. You're on the *Enterprise!"*

Chekov rushed to inject the crazed man with a hypospray. As the man slumped onto the table, Chekov quickly loaded another dose, just in case.

The reporter gasped for breath. "What was he talking about?"

Chekov shook his head just as a dazed woman bumped into him. She was dark-skinned and dressed in the exotic garb of the El-Aurians. He started to inject her with the hypospray, but he stopped. She didn't look violent, just confused.

"Guinan," she said weakly. She started to faint, and Chekov grabbed her before she hit the floor.

"It's going to be okay," he told her. "Here, just lie down." He guided her to a table.

Chekov didn't know how much time had passed. He and the two journalists continued to sedate the survivors and assure them they were safe. After a while he couldn't feel the ship shaking anymore, and he assumed that the captain had gotten them out of danger. He didn't know which captain had saved them, but he would've bet on Captain Kirk.

A comm panel beeped on, and he tapped it. "Chekov here."

"Scotty," said a glum voice. "Can you meet me at the deflector relays? Deck 15, Section 21 alpha."

"Certainly," answered Chekov. "But I'm a bit busy here. We've got a lot of disoriented people."

"This will only take a moment," answered the old engineer. "It's important, lad. There's been an accident."

Chekov stood beside Scotty on Deck 15, staring at a jagged hole that had been ripped out of the corridor. Beyond the twisted shards of metal, stars glimmered with unearthly beauty. Occasionally a piece of wreckage floated by, reminding him of the situation. If not for a forcefield that crackled with energy, he and Scotty would have been sucked into the void as well.

"What happened?" Chekov demanded.

"We had to simulate a photon torpedo with the deflector beams," said Scotty. "Captain Kirk rushed down here to adjust the relays. There was no one else to do it. I was busy on the transporter, and the captain felt that Captain Harriman should stay on the bridge."

The old Scotsman shook his head in disbelief. "We got away from it, but the hull was breached. Right here—where the captain was working. All alone."

"Have we searched for him?" asked Chekov. He ran to a nearby comm panel and pounded it. "Chekov to bridge!"

"Sulu here," came the answer.

"Listen," said Chekov desperately, "we need a complete sweep of the ship, inside and out!"

"I've checked the entire ship and surrounding space a dozen times," Demora Sulu answered patiently. "There is no sign of Captain Kirk."

Scotty sighed and shook his head. "I told you, lad."

"Thank you," said Chekov, turning off the comm panel, helpless.

With bitterness Scotty added, "Just a quick run around the block."

"I never thought it would end like this. . . ." Chekov's voice choked. "The captain . . . dead."

The old engineer squared his shoulders. "All things must end, Mr. Chekov."

CHAPTER 3

Seventy-eight years later a sailing vessel with three tall masts rode splendidly on the choppy waves. This was the original *Enterprise,* a wooden sailing ship; it had prowled the seas of Earth six hundred years earlier.

Captain Jean-Luc Picard breathed in the fresh, salty air. This was the life for him! Cut off from the admirals and Starfleet command, riding the sea and the wind wherever it took him. Overhead, the timbers creaked in the wind, and the sails billowed proudly.

He turned to his first officer. Like Beverly Crusher, Deanna Troi, Geordi La Forge, Data, and dozens of others, Will Riker was dressed in nineteenth-century sailing garb. He wore a full-dress naval uniform, complete with cocked hat, epaulettes, and leggings. Somehow, thought Picard, Commander Riker always looked a bit confined in period clothes, as if they never quite fit his broad shoulders.

"'I must go down to the sea again,'" quoted the captain. "'To the lonely sea and sky.' Imagine what it was like, Will. No engine, no computers—just the wind, the sea, and the stars to guide you."

Riker scowled. "Bad food. Brutal discipline." He gulped. "No women."

Picard laughed and raised his hand. "Bring out the prisoner!"

A holographic drummer began a loud drumroll, and Worf was pushed out a door onto the deck. He had heavy iron shackles on his hands and legs, and he clanked as he walked. But he looked proud, as a Klingon should.

Captain Picard shook a stern finger at him. "Mr. Worf, I always knew this day would come. Are you prepared to face the charges?"

When Worf didn't answer, Deanna Troi poked him in the side. "Answer him!" she barked.

"I am prepared," said Worf in a low voice.

Riker unrolled a large parchment scroll and began to read: "We, the officers and crew of the *U.S.S. Enterprise,* being of sound mind and judgment, hereby make the following charges against Lieutenant Worf.

"One, that he did knowingly and willfully perform above and beyond the call of duty on countless occasions. Two, that he has been a good and solid officer on this ship for one score less twelve years. And three, most seriously, that he has earned the respect and admiration of the entire crew!"

Riker grinned and put away the scroll.

Picard nodded solemnly. "There can be only one judgment for such crimes. I hereby promote you to the rank of Lieutenant Commander, with all the rights and privileges thereto! And may God have mercy on your soul."

Everyone on the swaying deck roared with approval, and Geordi began to remove Worf's leg irons. The Klingon looked relieved for a moment, but then he saw Commander Riker's smile.

"Extend the plank!" ordered Riker.

With loud cheers the crew pushed a narrow board out over the choppy seas. As the ship rolled and heaved, a dozen hands gripped Worf and pushed him toward the railing.

"I bet that water's freezing," said Deanna with satisfaction.

Beverly Crusher looked concerned. "Geordi, did

you remember to engage the holodeck safety program? I don't know if Klingons can swim."

"I'm not sure," answered Geordi with a wink. Worf furrowed the deep ridges of his forehead as he was pushed onto the plank.

Picard turned to Riker with a questioning look. "Don't you think you're taking this a little too far, Number One?"

Riker grinned. "When we went to ancient Rome for Deanna's promotion, we threw her to the lions. Remember?"

Picard smiled and turned his attention back to the plank.

"Lower the Badge of Office!" called Riker.

A crewman on the yardarm lowered a rope with a hat at the end of it. It was a grand officer's hat with a feathered plume, and he dangled it over the end of the plank.

"You can do it, Worf!" somebody shouted. "Don't look down!"

The big Klingon grunted at the encouragement and took a deep breath. Then he ran to the end of the plank and made a spectacular leap into the air. The crewman yanked the hat, but Worf grabbed it with one hand and landed back on the plank. He teetered for a moment, the board groaning under his weight. Just as it seemed Worf would maintain his balance, Riker gestured for the plank to be removed—and Worf plummeted into the water. The splash was like the spume from a whale, and the crowd cheered with delight.

Data stepped between Captain Picard and Dr. Crusher, who were both laughing out loud. The gold-skinned android leaned over the railing to watch Worf struggle in the icy sea.

"Doctor," said the android, "I must confess I am uncertain why someone falling into freezing water is amusing."

"It's all in good fun, Data," answered Beverly.

He looked at her blankly. "I do not under-stand."

"Try to get in the spirit of things," said Beverly. "Learn to be a little more spontaneous."

Data thought for a moment, then he pushed Beverly over the rail into the dark waters. She hit with a big splash, but nobody laughed.

"Data," said Geordi sternly, "that wasn't funny."

However, thought Picard, the expression on Data's face was very funny as he tried to understand his mistake. The captain waved to Riker. "Number One, bring the ship before the wind. Let's see what's out there."

Before Riker could give the order to jibe into the

wind, a voice broke into the proceedings. "Bridge to Captain Picard."

The captain sighed. "Picard here."

"There's a personal message for you from Earth."

"Put it through down here," answered Picard. He stepped away from the excitement to a quiet corner of the deck. "Computer," he ordered, "arch."

As if by magic, a U-shaped arch with computer panels suddenly became visible. From where she was standing at the helm, Deanna Troi could see Captain Picard reading a text message. She couldn't read the exact words, but she could see the pained expression on his face.

"Take the wheel," she said to a nearby crewman. She strode to the captain's side and whispered, "Captain, are you all right?"

He nodded, but his mind was elsewhere. "Yes, fine, Counselor. If you'll excuse me. Computer, exit."

The holodeck door appeared, and the captain wandered off. Riker walked to Deanna's side and gave her a concerned look. Suddenly another voice came from the comm panel.

"Bridge to Commander Riker."

"Riker here," he answered.

"We're picking up a distress call from the Amargosa Observatory, sir. They say they're under attack."

"Red alert!" barked the commander. "All hands to Battlestations! Captain Picard to the bridge."

Deanna Troi was certain that the captain would beat them to the bridge. He always did, in a crisis. But he was nowhere in sight when the bridge crew arrived at their stations. They got some funny looks from the relief crew, because they were still wearing their sailing costumes.

Within seconds of arriving in the Amargosa system, all eyes were on the viewscreen. They could see the immense solar observatory, with its complex array of telescopes and sensors—now blackened and burned out. The only sign of life came from the giant yellow sun in the distance. It throbbed with a million times the energy of Sol, Earth's sun.

"It looks as if we're too late," muttered Riker.

"There are no other ships in this system," reported Worf.

"Searching for lifesigns," said Data as his fingers breezed over the ops console.

Captain Picard finally stepped out of his ready room. To Deanna, he still didn't look engaged in the action. He half listened as Riker filled him in.

"Survivors?" asked Picard.

Data nodded. "Sensors show five lifesigns aboard the station, Captain."

Riker added, "The station complement was nineteen."

"Stand down from red alert," said Picard. "Number One, begin the investigation."

"Sir, I thought that you would—"

"Make it so," growled Picard, marching back to his ready room. "Do it."

Riker nodded, and Deanna felt bad for Will. If the captain wanted to be left out of it, that was his business. It was also *her* business, but she would have to deal with it later.

Riker turned to Worf. "We'll need armed security for the away team. Worf, you're with me. You, too, Dr. Crusher."

CHAPTER 4

Riker, Worf, Beverly, and two security officers materialized on the main deck of the solar observatory. The station was a burned wreck—consoles flickered and sparked, and acrid smoke spewed into the air. When the lights dimmed, the security officers turned on their hand-held beams and kept their phasers ready.

Riker picked his way carefully around the twisted metal and blown-out consoles. Scorch marks were everywhere. *Someone has sure taken target practice to this place,* he thought. The commander couldn't see anything worth saving, and he waited for Worf and Beverly to check their tricorders.

Worf reported, "These blast patterns are consistent with type-three disruptors."

"Well," said Riker, "that narrows it to Klingon, Breen, or Romulan."

Beverly moved past them, intent upon her medical tricorder. "I'm picking up lifesigns . . . about twenty meters ahead."

"That rules out Klingons," said Worf.

When Riker gave him a quizzical look, Worf added, "They would not have left anyone alive."

"Over here!" called Beverly.

She rushed as fast as she could through the debris and uncovered an injured Starfleet officer. He had a nasty-looking burn across his back, the result of a disruptor beam. As the doctor opened her med-kit and set to work on the wounded officer, Riker looked around the station.

"Worf," he said, "you're with me. Paskall, you and Mendez search the upper deck."

The security officers dashed to a nearby ladder and began to climb. Worf turned on his light beam, and Riker followed it into a dark corridor. They found two bodies sprawled on the deck, and Riker bent over them to check for lifesigns. He shook his head a second later—they had both taken disruptor blasts at point-blank range.

There was a sudden banging from behind a collapsed bulkhead, and Riker jumped to his feet. He reached the wreckage before Worf and tried to lift it himself, but it was just too heavy. Once the big Klingon put his brawn into the job, the sheet of metal began to move. Riker could see a pair of legs underneath.

They heard the man gasping for air, and that made their fingers move faster as they dug through the rubble. The survivor eagerly gripped Worf's hands and tried to claw his way out.

He was wild-eyed, and he had a scar on his head from a wound many years earlier.

"It is all right," Worf assured him. "Do not struggle."

Riker bent down to try to calm the man. "I'm Commander William Riker of the *Starship Enterprise.*"

"Soran," the man croaked. "Dr. Tolian Soran . . ."

"Who attacked you, Doctor?"

"I'm not sure. It happened so fast . . ."

They heard footsteps in the corridor and turned to see Dr. Crusher and one of the security officers. "Commander!" he called. "You'd better take a look at this."

"You attend to him, Dr. Crusher," said Riker.

Worf and the commander got up and followed the security officer to the ladder. A few seconds later he found himself on the upper deck, where the carnage was just as bad as below. There were several charred bodies in view, but the officer led him to one in particular. When he turned it over, Riker caught his breath.

The dead man had distinctive pointed ears, a widow's peak hairline, and an exotic uniform with large shoulders.

A Romulan.

Data sat in a chair in his quarters, his cat nestled in his lap. He petted Spot without giving it much thought, because the cat enjoyed it. Why, he wondered, do humans find it comforting to give affection to a small mammal? He didn't know why, but he wished he could experience the feeling.

The android had gotten a pet several years earlier, as an experiment in human behavior. He hadn't learned anything about humans, but he had learned a lot about cats. He even knew how to successfully raise a litter of kittens.

His door chimed. "Come!" he called.

It *whooshed* open, and his friend Geordi rushed in. The chief engineer of the *Enterprise* didn't look very happy, even with his VISOR hiding his eyes.

"Is she still angry?" asked the android.

Geordi shook his head. "I don't think so, but I'd stay out of sickbay for a while, if I were you. Whatever made you push her into the water?"

The android cocked his head. "I was attempting to . . . get into the spirit of things. I thought it would be amusing."

Data set Spot down, stood, and walked to his desk. He had made a decision. It seemed like the only way. He activated a control panel, and a small compartment slid open. Inside was a computer chip, in a clear antistatic case. It was beautiful, in its own way.

Geordi moved beside him. "Data," he said with concern, "are you really thinking about using that thing?"

"I have considered it for many months," answered the android. "In light of the incident with Dr. Crusher, I believe this may be a good time."

"I thought you were afraid it would overload your neural net."

Data turned to Geordi. "My growth as an artifical life-form has reached an impasse. For thirty-four years I have tried to become more human, to grow beyond my original programming. Yet I am still unable to grasp such a basic concept as humor."

He lifted the chip from the hidden compartment and gazed at it. "This emotion chip may be the only answer. Will you help me?"

"Yeah," answered Geordi with reluctance. "But at the first sign of trouble, I'm going to deactivate it. Agreed?"

Data nodded. "Agreed." He expected nothing less from his friend.

Data experienced no real sensation as Geordi opened up Data's head, revealing a mass of blinking circuits. He was aware of a slight power fluctuation when the chip was installed. Otherwise, Data didn't feel any different.

"I do not feel any emotions," said Data.

"Neither do I," answered Geordi. "You don't feel emotions all the time. Come on, let's go down to Ten-Forward."

The ship's lounge was bustling with people, and Data felt a moment of confusion as he and Geordi entered. How was he supposed to deal with all these people? What was he going to say to them? The android felt better after he remembered that fear of crowded places was a common human emotion. The chip seemed to be working.

Geordi was watching him closely, and that made him a bit nervous, too. He moved swiftly to the bar, and Geordi followed. They were greeted by a big grin from Guinan, the dark-skinned woman who was in charge of Ten-Forward.

She set a bottle containing a dark liquid on the bar and told them, "You two just volunteered to be my first victims. This is a new drink I picked up on Forcas Three. Trust me, you're going to love it."

She poured two glasses of the liquid. While Geordi watched, Data picked up his glass and took a sniff. He felt suspicious of the liquid, but he drank it to be polite.

A moment later a disgusted look swept across Data's face. "I believe this beverage has provoked an emotional response," he said.

Geordi leaned forward. "Really? What do you feel?"

Data shook his head. "I . . . I am uncertain. I am unable to articulate the sensation. I have little experience with emotions."

"Emotions?" asked Guinan.

"I'll explain later," said Geordi. "Go on, Data, try some more."

Both of them watched intently as Data finished his drink. The android frowned in thought, trying to put words to what he was feeling.

"I think he hates it," said Guinan.

"Yes, that is it!" exclaimed Data with excitement. "I *hate* it. It is revolting!"

Guinan smiled. "Another round?"

Data nodded eagerly. "Please!"

Commander Riker loudly cleared his throat. He didn't normally have to do that when addressing the captain, but the captain wasn't paying attention. He was staring out the window of his ready room, and his mind was light-years away,

Picard heard the noise and turned to face his first officer. "You were saying, Number One?

"Yes, sir. We found two dead Romulans aboard the station. We're checking their equipment to see if we can determine what ship they came from."

Picard asked, "Is there any indication why they attacked the station?"

"Not yet," answered Riker, "but they tore the place apart. They accessed the central computer and turned the cargo bay inside out. They must have been looking for something."

Picard shrugged, as if this news wasn't very interesting. "Inform Starfleet Command," he said. "This could indicate a new Romulan threat in this sector."

Riker blinked in amazement. "You want *me* to contact Starfleet?"

"Is there a problem?" the captain asked curtly.

"No, sir."

"Thank you, Number One."

Riker started for the door, then stopped. "There is something else, Captain. One of the scientists, a Dr. Soran, says he has to speak with you. I told him you were busy, but he said it was urgent."

Picard was looking out the window again. "Understood. That will be all."

Riker knew he should leave. The captain obviously wanted to be left alone with his thoughts. But a Federation station had been destroyed in a mysterious attack, and there were Romulans involved. This was not the time for the captain to be preoccupied. Plus, Captain Picard was his friend.

"Sir," asked Riker, "is there anything wrong?"

The captain's face was like a mask. "No," he answered. "Where is this Dr. Soran?"

"Ten-Forward," answered Riker.

"I'll go see him."

A few moments later Captain Picard entered the Ten-Forward lounge and looked around. The captain knew he couldn't sit alone and stare out the window forever. Perhaps it would be good for him to be around people, he thought. But after hearing the laughter and the good cheer, he almost turned around and left. This was not the place for him.

Then he saw a man seated alone at a table. He was wearing a distinctive uniform, much different from a Starfleet uniform. He looked as troubled as Picard, so the captain walked toward him.

"Dr. Soran?" he asked.

The man stood up and nodded. "Yes, yes, Captain. Thank you for coming."

The men shook hands, and Picard sat down, waiting to hear what was so urgent. Soran was a bundle of nervous energy. *Of course,* thought Picard, *having your station attacked might make anyone nervous.*

Soran leaned forward. "Captain, I need to return to the observatory immediately. I must continue a critical experiment I was running on the Amargosa star."

The captain's lips thinned. Even when he was in a good mood, he didn't like to be told what to do. "We're still investigating the attack," he answered. "Once we've completed our work, we'll be happy to allow you to go back. Until then—"

"No," said Soran, interrupting him. "The timing is very important on my experiment. If it is not completed within the next twelve hours, years of research will be lost!"

Picard shook his head. "We're doing the best we can. Now if you'll excuse me."

When the captain stood to leave, Soran suddenly grabbed his arm. Picard could feel the strength in his grip, and he stared into Soran's wild blue eyes.

"Captain, they say that time is the fire in which we burn. Right now my time is running out."

The scientist let go of Picard's arm as he tried to explain. "We leave so many things unfinished in our lives. Do you understand what I'm saying?"

Picard swallowed hard. He understood exactly what Dr. Soran was saying. Those were the same thoughts he was wrestling with. *So many things unfinished. . . .*

The captain's voice was a whisper. "I'll see what I can do," he said, turning to go.

Picard wondered why fate had brought Dr. Soran to the *Enterprise*. It was strange that both of them were so worried about time running out. It had already run out for Captain Picard, and he wanted to help Dr. Soran if he could.

A young ensign at a nearby table laughed just then, and he looked at her as he passed. When she saw the captain's stern expression, she grew quiet. He wanted to tell the young ensign to keep laughing, to live her life to the fullest. When it was gone, it was gone forever.

But he just lowered his head and walked away.

Soran sat for a few more minutes, staring at Guinan on the other side of the lounge, serving drinks. Nobody could miss her in her outlandish hat.

He took an antique pocket watch out of his uniform and gazed at it for several seconds. Then he stood and walked briskly toward the door.

CHAPTER

Geordi La Forge stood on the main deck of the solar observatory, marveling at the wreckage. This was his first trip to the station, and he found it hard to believe. It was almost as if vandals had struck the place, destroying just to destroy.

Data was with him, and the android walked swiftly around the room with his tricorder. Geordi was about to turn on his own tricorder when his comm badge beeped.

He tapped it. "La Forge here."

He recognized Commander Riker's voice. "Geordi, we finally have something to go on. Worf has analyzed the Romulans' sensor logs, and we think they were looking for particles of trilithium."

"Trilithium?" asked Geordi. "That's a compound the Romulans have been working on for years. In theory they could make an explosive that would be more powerful than antimatter. But they could never stabilize it. And why would they look for it *here?"*

"I don't know," answered Riker. "But they were looking for it, and so should we. Riker out."

Geordi turned on his tricorder. "Did you hear that, Data? Scan for particles of trilithium."

Data suddenly started to giggle. "I get it! I get it!"

"You get what?"

Data laughed even harder, almost doubling over. "When you said to Commander Riker, 'The clown can stay, but the Ferengi in the gorilla suit has to go.'"

Geordi just stared at the amused android. "What?"

"You must remember," said Data. "It was during the Farpoint mission. We were on the bridge, and you told a joke. That was a very good punchline."

"The Farpoint mission? Data, that was *seven years* ago!"

Data smiled proudly. "I know. I just got it. Very amusing."

Geordi shrugged. "Thanks. We'd better start our search, or Commander Riker won't be laughing."

The engineer moved down a corridor, with the chuckling android following him. Suddenly Geordi stopped in front of what looked like a standard bulkhead. It fooled the tricorder, but it didn't fool Geordi's enhanced visual instrument.

"Data," he said, "there's a hidden doorway here. I can see the joints in the metal with my VISOR." He ran his fingers along what looked like solid metal but wasn't.

Data studied his tricorder. "There appears to be a dampening field in operation. I cannot scan beyond the bulkhead."

Geordi put his tricorder back on his belt and ran his hands across the bulkhead. "There must be a control panel. Or an access port."

"Allow me," said Data. He opened a small panel on his wrist and made a quick adjustment to his inner circuitry. "It appears to be magnetically sealed. However, I believe I can reverse the polarity by attenuating my axial servo."

Finished, Data closed the panel on his wrist and touched the wall. "Open sesame," he said.

There was a humming sound, followed by a loud click. The hidden door slid open.

Data grinned. "You could say I have a magnetic personality." He chuckled at his own joke.

There was a small room beyond the door, and Geordi entered cautiously. At first glance it was nothing more than a storage room for solar probes. Several of the shiny spheres were stacked in holding racks.

Geordi took out his tricorder and began scanning again. "Somebody went to a lot of trouble to shield this room. But I'm not picking up anything unusual." He stopped. "What's this?"

The engineer bent down to inspect a probe that had several odd devices attached to its side. "Data, have you ever seen a solar probe like this?"

The android grinned and held up his tricorder. Speaking in a squeaky voice, he opened and closed the tricorder as if it were a puppet's mouth. "No, Geordi, I have not. Have you?"

Data laughed at himself, and Geordi sighed. His patience with the new, emotional Data was running out. "Just help me get this panel open, okay?"

The android bent down and swiftly opened a panel on the side of the probe. Geordi jumped back as if he had been slapped.

"Whoa!" he gasped. "My VISOR's picking up something in the theta band. It could be trilithium."

Data started howling with laughter. Geordi turned and snapped at him, "Data, this is not the time!"

Between belly laughs, the android said, "I am sorry . . . I cannot stop myself. . . . I think something is wrong."

As Geordi watched in horror, Data's laughter turned into hysteria. Then Data began to jerk and shake like a man going through convulsions. In a matter of seconds a rush of emotions raced across his face—everything from anger to passion. Then the android went stiff and fell to the floor of the storage room.

"Data!" Geordi shouted. He bent over his friend and looked at him for signs of damage. The android suddenly blinked and opened his eyes.

"Are you all right?" asked Geordi.

Data jerked his head. "I believe the emotion chip has overloaded my positronic relays."

"We'd better get you back to the ship." Geordi hit his comm badge. "La Forge to *Enterprise.*"

There was no answer. His comm badge was dead. Geordi was about to take his badge off and check it when he heard a voice from the doorway.

"Is there a problem, gentlemen?"

Geordi turned to see Dr. Soran. "Oh, it's you," he said with relief. "As a matter of fact, we do have a problem. Data needs assistance, and the dampening field in here is blocking our comm signal."

But Dr. Soran wasn't listening. He was looking past Geordi at the solar probe they had opened. A troubled look crossed his face, then he was calm again.

"I'd be happy to help you."

Data felt relief, knowing that Dr. Soran would aid

him. After all, this was the doctor's station. He would know how to turn off the dampening field.

Soran bent down as if to help, but his hand turned into a fist! He punched Geordi so hard that the engineer reeled backward, and his VISOR flew off his face. It clattered to a stop in a corner of the room. Geordi didn't move—he was unconscious.

Data tried to get up, but Dr. Soran was pointing a disruptor weapon at him. Fear overwhelmed the android.

"Please do not hurt me," begged Data.

Deanna Troi stood outside Captain Picard's quarters. She paced, slamming her fist into her palm. Even though she had served a long time with the captain, she never found it easy to counsel him. He was a good man, an excellent man, but he was also a private man. He could be difficult, when he wanted to be.

She squared her shoulders and chimed his door.

"Come!" said a deep voice.

The door *whooshed* open, and she entered. His quarters were not luxurious, but they were tasteful. On the walls and shelves were many mementos of his adventures and visits to strange planets. The captain was sitting at his desk, holding something she had never seen before.

It was a photo album.

He sniffed and rubbed his nose. "Counselor. What can I do for you?"

"Actually," she said, "I'm here to see if I can do anything for you. You've seemed a little distracted lately."

The captain looked at her for several moments. He seemed to be making up his mind about something, and he finally said, "Just some family matters. You've never met my brother and his wife, have you?"

He turned the photo album around so she could see it, and she moved closer. The album was opened to a page showing a stern-faced man and a friendly-looking woman. Seated with them was a handsome boy. Several other photos showed a charming farm-house and rows of vines. Grapevines, she remem-bered. Jean-Luc Picard had grown up on a vineyard in France.

The resemblance between the captain and his brother was obvious. They both looked like men who were used to getting their way.

Picard sniffed again. "Robert can be quite impossi-ble. Pompous, arrogant—he always has to have the last word. But he's mellowed somewhat in his later years." He shook his head. "I was planning to spend some time on Earth next month. I thought we could

43

all go to San Francisco. His son, René, has always wanted to see Starfleet Academy."

Troi looked again at the photo of the boy. "Your nephew?"

The captain smiled fondly. "Yes. He's so unlike his father. He's imaginative, a dreamer. He reminds me of myself at that age."

"Captain, what's happened?"

Picard took a deep breath and looked away. For the first time Deanna felt the depth of his pain. He was a private man, but he couldn't hide this.

"That message from Earth," said the captain. "Robert and René . . . they're dead. They were burned to death in a fire."

Deanna tried to appear calm, but the captain's grief swept over her. He seemed to sense it as he rose to his feet and looked out the window.

"I'm so sorry," she finally said.

He shrugged. "It's all right. These things happen. We all have our time, and theirs came."

"No, it's not all right," said the counselor. "And the sooner you realize that, the sooner you can come to terms with what happened."

"I know that," answered Picard. "It's not me I feel sorry for. It's my nephew. I just can't stop thinking about him—about all the experiences he'll never have. Going to the Academy, falling in love, having children of his own. It's all gone."

"I had no idea he meant so much to you."

The captain nodded. "He was as close as I ever came to having a child of my own. We all lived for that boy."

"Your family history is very important to you, isn't it?" asked Deanna.

"Yes," said the captain. "Ever since I was a little boy, I remember hearing about the family line. The Picards that fought at Trafalgar, the Picards that settled the first Martian colony. When my brother married and had a son . . ." The captain stopped, as if he couldn't continue.

Deanna ended his thought. "You felt that you didn't have to have children of your own, to carry on the family line."

"My brother did that for me," he admitted. "It allowed me to pursue my own selfish needs."

"There's nothing selfish about having your own life and career," said Deanna.

The captain took a deep breath. "You know, Counselor, my life is half over. There are fewer days ahead of me than there are behind me. But I always took comfort in the fact that when I was gone, my family would continue. But now . . ."

Captain Picard reached for the photo album and turned to the last page. It was blank. In anger and grief he slammed his fist on the table.

"After this the idea of death is so *real* to me! When I die, there will be no more Picards."

Deanna tried to think of what to say. She could tell the captain that he was still young enough to have children, if he had a wife. But she knew that being captain of the *Enterprise* was not a job for a family man.

Suddenly a burst of light flashed through the window and flooded the room. It was so bright that both of them had to shield their eyes against the glare.

Riker's voice sounded over the communication system. "Senior officers report to the bridge! All hands to duty stations!"

CHAPTER

6

Captain Picard strode off the turbolift onto the bridge of the *Enterprise*. Counselor Troi was right behind him. Commander Riker was glad to see them both, but there was no time for greetings. On the viewscreen the once vibrant Amargosa star was growing darker by the moment, and a mass of flaming debris was headed their way.

"Report," snapped Picard.

Riker answered, "A quantum implosion has occurred within the Amargosa star. All nuclear fusion is breaking down."

"How is that possible?" asked the captain.

Worf reported, "Sensor records show the observatory launched a solar probe into the sun a few moments ago."

"The star's going to collapse in a matter of minutes," added Riker.

"Captain," said Worf with concern, "the implosion has produced a level-twelve shock wave."

"Level twelve!" gasped Deanna. "That'll destroy everything in this system."

A voice broke in. "Transporter room to bridge. I can't locate Commander La Forge or Mr. Data!"

Riker turned to Worf. "Did they return to the ship?"

"No, sir," answered the Klingon, working his console. "They are not aboard."

Picard demanded, "How long until the shock wave hits the observatory?"

"Four minutes, forty seconds," answered Worf.

Picard looked at Riker, and the first officer nodded. He knew what he had to do as he rushed for the turbolift.

"Mr. Worf," he barked, "with me!"

Seconds later Riker and Worf were prowling the main deck of the observatory, searching for Data and Geordi. They went through room after room as quickly as they could until they came upon Dr. Soran. The scientist was watching the star's collapse on his instrument panel. When he heard them, he whirled around and fired his disruptor.

The blast took off a chunk of the bulkhead, and

Riker and Worf ducked for cover. "What's he doing?" growled Riker.

"He must have set off the probe," answered Worf. He peered cautiously around the corner. "I see La Forge. He is not moving." Another disruptor blast drilled into the wall, forcing the Klingon to hit the deck.

Captain Picard's voice cut in. *"Enterprise* to Commander Riker. You have two minutes left."

"Acknowledged," said Riker. Then he shouted, "Soran! Did you hear that? There's a level-twelve shock wave coming. We've got to get out of here!"

Soran's only answer was another disruptor shot.

"Enterprise to Riker," came the captain's voice. "A Klingon Bird of Prey has just decloaked off our port bow."

"What?" growled Worf.

"We have to get you back here," insisted Picard.

"Acknowledged," said Riker. Something had caught his eye, and he peered around the corner to get a better look. There was Data, huddled in a corner, shivering with fear.

"Data!" called Riker. "See if you can get to Geordi!"

The android looked at him with sheer terror. "I . . . I cannot, sir. I am afraid."

Suddenly another communicator beeped, only farther away. Riker and Worf crept out of hiding to see Soran moving away from his instruments. Geordi was still unconscious, but Soran grabbed him by the collar and lifted him up. In his other hand he held Geordi's VISOR.

A moment later Soran and Geordi vanished in a column of dazzling light.

Worf snarled, "They transported to the Klingon ship!"

"Enterprise to away team," said Captain Picard. "The Klingon ship is gone, and we have no more time."

Riker and Worf rushed to Data's side, and they lifted the frightened android to his feet. "Three to transport," said Riker. "When ready."

The three of them disappeared in a swirl of colored lights. A few seconds later the entire observatory disappeared in searing flames.

On the Klingon Bird of Prey, Lursa and B'Etor were laughing at the way they had outwitted the mighty *Enterprise.* They were sisters—strong, powerful Klingon women. They had beaten the Federation before, but never this well.

"Well done!" Lursa said to her Klingon crew. The men cheered, and she grinned at them. Their ship was old and patched up in many places, but it was still battle-ready. With their new weapon, they would be invincible!

B'Etor watched the viewscreen. She smiled at the way the collapsed sun destroyed its solar system. "Glorious," she said.

Dr. Soran strode from the turbolift onto the bridge of the Klingon ship. B'Etor rushed to greet him.

"Excellent, Soran!" She beamed. "We have done it!"

Without warning the scientist slugged the Klingon woman in the jaw. She went sprawling onto the deck. The Klingon crewmen leaped to their feet, drawing their weapons. But B'Etor held up her hand as she struggled to her feet. There was a trickle of blood at the corner of her mouth.

She hissed, "I hope for your sake, Soran, that you are initiating a game."

"You got careless," he snapped. "The Romulans came looking for their missing trilithium."

B'Etor shook her head. "Impossible. We left no survivors on their outpost."

"Lucky for us the *Enterprise* scared them off," said Soran.

"What does it matter?" asked Lursa. "We now have a weapon of unlimited power!"

"I have the weapon," Soran insisted. "If you want me to give it to you, you had better be more careful in the future." He turned to go.

B'Etor suddenly jumped Soran from behind and stuck a knife to his throat. "Perhaps we are tired of waiting."

Soran didn't move. He only smiled. "Without my research, the trilithium is worthless. So are your plans to reconquer the Klingon Empire."

This isn't getting us anywhere, thought Lursa. She pushed her sister's knife away from Soran's throat.

"We are partners," she cooed. "And Soran has brought us a hostage." She turned to the helmsman. "Set course for the Veridian system. Maximum warp."

Dr. Soran straightened his collar. "Have someone bring Commander Geordi La Forge to my quarters. I need some answers from him."

Commander Riker walked down the corridor toward sickbay. He tried not to think about losing Geordi, or letting Soran get away. Most of all, he tried not to think about Data, cowering with fear.

"Commander Riker!" called a deep voice. He turned to see Worf headed toward him.

"I have spoken to the Klingon High Council," said Worf. "They identified the Bird of Prey as belonging to the Duras sisters." He said their name with contempt.

Riker blinked with surprise. "Lursa and B'Etor? This doesn't make any sense. A renowned scientist uses a trilithium probe to destroy a star. Then he kidnaps Geordi and escapes with a pair of Klingon renegades. Why? What is he getting out of it?"

Worf could only shake his head in reply. They entered sickbay and found Dr. Beverly Crusher working on Data's head. The android was awake, scanning himself with a tricorder.

"How is he?" asked Riker.

Beverly sighed. "It looks as if a power surge fused the emotion chip into his neural net."

"Will that be a danger to him?" asked Worf.

"I don't think so," answered Beverly. "The chip is still working, but I can't remove it without taking apart his cerebral conduit. I'm not sure I want to try it, without Geordi to help me."

Riker tried to smile at Data. "It looks as if you're stuck with emotions for a while. How do you feel?"

"I am quite concerned about Geordi," admitted the android.

"We all are, Data. But we're going to get him back."

The android frowned. "I hope so, sir."

"Commander," said Beverly, "I checked into Dr. Soran's background." She activated a screen on the wall behind her, and Soran's picture appeared, along with information about him.

She went on, "He's an El-Aurian, over three hundred years old. He lost his entire family when the Borg destroyed his world. Soran escaped with a handful of other refugees aboard a ship called the *Lakul*. That ship was destroyed by some kind of energy ribbon, but Soran and forty-six others were rescued by the *Enterprise-B*."

"Wasn't that the mission where Captain James Kirk was killed?" asked Riker.

"Yes," said Beverly, "but that's not all. I checked the passenger list of the *Lakul*. Someone else we know was on that ship. Guinan."

The commander nodded thoughtfully. "Nobody knows Guinan as well as the captain. He should be the one to talk to her."

Captain Picard stood in the center of Guinan's quarters, looking down at her. The El-Aurian sat cross-legged on the floor, surrounded by exotic-looking pillows. Strange fabrics and artwork hung on the walls, and the lighting was dim and peaceful.

Guinan was a mystery to everyone, but to him she was a familiar mystery. He had known her for many years, and it had been at his request that she came to serve aboard the *Enterprise*. That was a decision he had never regretted.

"There's a man we think you know," said Picard. "Dr. Tolian Soran."

Guinan was a hard one to surprise, but she stared at him in amazement. "That's a name I haven't heard in a long time," she answered. She stood and walked away from Picard, as if she didn't want to say anything else.

"Guinan," he insisted, "it's very important that you tell us what you know about him. We think he's developed a weapon—a terrible weapon. Could he be seeking power?"

She smiled wistfully. "Soran doesn't care about power, or weapons. All he cares about is getting back to the nexus."

The captain had a sinking feeling in his stomach. He had never questioned Guinan about her powers, her ability to know things she shouldn't know. But he felt as if he would get close to the truth with his next question.

"What's the nexus?" he asked.

Guinan moved away from him again and rearranged the articles on a table. She was considering her answer, and he waited patiently.

"The energy ribbon that destroyed the *Lakul* isn't

some random thing," she answered. "It's a doorway. It leads to another place—the nexus. It doesn't exist in our universe, and it doesn't play by the same rules, either. It's a place I've tried very hard to forget."

"What happened to you?"

She turned to him, and her face was filled with awe and happiness at the memory. "It was like being inside . . . joy. As if joy were a real thing I could wrap around myself. I've never been so content."

"Until the *Enterprise*-B rescued you," said Picard.

Guinan showed a rare burst of anger. "I didn't want to leave. None of us did. For a long time all I could think about was getting back. I didn't care what I had to do."

She looked out her window at the glimmer of stars in the distance. "I learned to live with it, but it changed me."

Picard nodded. "Your sixth sense. And what about Soran?"

"He may still be obsessed with getting back. If he is, he'll do anything to find that doorway again."

The captain had many other questions, but he doubted if Guinan could answer them. Only Soran could.

"Thank you, Guinan." He started toward the door.

"Jean-Luc," she said with a warning in her voice. "Let someone else stop him. If you go into that nexus,

Captain Montgomery "Scotty" Scott (James Doohan) is shocked at Captain Kirk's (William Shatner) refusal to attend the christening of the *U.S.S. Enterprise* 1701-B.

On the *U.S.S. Enterprise* 1701-B, Captain Kirk and Commander Pavel Chekov (Walter Koenig) prepare to greet an old friend.

Captain Kirk takes command of the *Enterprise*-B to answer a distress call.

Ensign Demora Sulu (Jacqueline Kim) and Captain Harriman (Alan Ruck) struggle to stabilize the *Enterprise*-B.

Aboard the good ship *Enterprise*, Captain Jean-Luc Picard (Patrick Stewart) and Commander William Riker (Jonathan Frakes) announce Lieutenant Worf's promotion.

Security Chief Worf (Michael Dorn) proudly accepts his promotion.

Chief Engineer Geordi La Forge (LeVar Burton) explains to Commander Data (Brent Spiner) why they made Worf walk the plank.

Guinan (Whoopi Goldberg) senses the presence of Dr. Soran.

In Stellar Cartography, Captain Picard and Commander Data investigate an interspatial nexus.

Dr. Beverly Crusher (Gates McFadden) examines Commander Data's malfunctioning emotion chip.

The Duras sisters, Lursa (Barbara March) and B'Etor (Gwynyth Walsh) face off against the *U.S.S. Enterprise.*

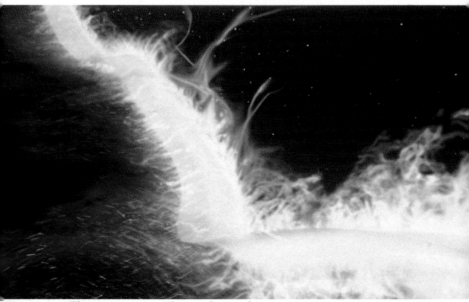

The nexus rips through a solar system.

Captain Picard asks Captain Kirk for help.

Captain Kirk fights for his life against Dr. Soran.

With First Officer Riker in command, Counselor Deanna Troi (Marina Sirtis) takes charge of Navigation.

Commander Data is happy to find his cat, Spot, alive and well.

you're not going to care about Soran, or the *Enterprise,* or anyone. All you're going to care about is how it feels to be there. And you're never going to come back."

Picard looked at her, sensing the truth in her warning. Already he didn't care about anything. He was numb with grief over the death of his brother and his young nephew. Only his sense of duty was making him care about anything.

"I'll worry about that when the time comes," he said.

Geordi La Forge had no idea what the room looked like where he was held prisoner. He was blind without his VISOR. He knew the room smelled bad, like dirt and smoke. A slight hum told him that he was on a ship, headed somewhere. All of that wouldn't be so bad, but he hated being the prisoner of a madman.

And Dr. Soran was a madman. Geordi didn't need his VISOR to tell him that. He didn't expect to live through the day, but he was determined to die bravely.

"Let's try to move beyond the usual banter," said Dr. Soran. "I've got your VISOR, and I might be willing to give it back, if you answer a few questions. Why were you searching for trilithium on my station?"

"I was ordered to," answered Geordi. If the truth was harmless, he would be happy to tell it.

"I'm an El-Aurian," said Soran. "Some people call us a race of Listeners. We listen. Right now, Mr. La Forge, you have my undivided attention. I want to listen to everything you know about trilithium. And me. What did Guinan tell you about me?"

"Guinan? I don't know what you're talking about."

A sudden pain grabbed his chest and squeezed him like a vise. He couldn't breath, and it felt as if someone were stabbing him! Geordi tried not to scream, but he flopped in his chair like a fish on the ground. This was it—he was dying!

As suddenly as it started, the pain stopped. He slumped back in his chair. There was nothing to do but wait . . . wait until Soran killed him.

"Oh," said Soran, "I forgot to tell you. While you were asleep, I injected a nano-probe into your bloodstream. It's been navigating your cardiovascular system, and right now I've attached it to your heart. It's a little trick I picked up from the Borg."

Geordi's throat was raw, and he could barely speak. But he wasn't going to let this madman know it. "Yeah," he rasped, "the Borg are full of great ideas."

"I just stopped your heart for five seconds," said the madman. "It felt like an eternity, didn't it? Did you know that you can stop the human heart for up to six minutes before you get brain damage?"

"No. I didn't know that."

Soran chuckled. "We learn something new about ourselves every day. Maybe I didn't make myself clear. It is very important that you tell me exactly what Captain Picard knows about me and the trilithium."

"I told you everything. You might as well just kill me right now."

Soran's voice was angry. "I'm not a killer, Mr. La Forge. Let's try thirty seconds."

The pain threw Geordi out of his chair, and he fell onto the floor. This time he screamed, and kept on screaming.

CHAPTER 7

Captain Picard paced the central platform of the stellar cartography room. This was one part of the *Enterprise* he rarely visited, because he had done enough star-charting early in his career. But the cartography screens were the only ones large enough to show the nexus as it moved through the galaxy, and through time.

He and Data were surrounded by vast screens, full of stars. Some displayed distant sectors of space; others showed stars as they existed centuries earlier. The strange ribbon of energy called the nexus snaked among these stars like a living thing. But it wasn't the *real* nexus, only a computer simulation.

The captain kept glancing at Data, hoping he would hurry up. The android sat at the computer console, entering data and studying the results. He looked distracted, lost in thought. When he saw the captain looking at him, he straightened up in his chair and punched the console with flying fingers.

"According to our information," said Data, "the ribbon is a conflux of temporal energy. It travels through our galaxy every thirty-nine-point-one years. It will pass through this sector in approximately forty-two hours."

The captain looked grim at the news. It meant that Guinan was right. Soran's actions were tied to the nexus and his desire to get back to it.

"Soran destroyed the Amargosa star for some reason," said Picard. "Give me a list of anything which has been affected by the star's destruction. It doesn't matter how small."

Data stared ahead, as if he was daydreaming.

"Data!" snapped the captain.

The android snapped out of it and entered more commands. "Sorry, sir. It will take the computer a few moments to compile the information."

As he waited, Data sighed and lowered his head. He looked very gloomy, thought Picard.

"Are you all right?" asked the captain.

"No, sir. I am finding it difficult to concentrate. I believe I am overwhelmed with feelings of regret. Over my actions on the observatory."

"What do you mean?"

Data shook his head in disbelief. "I wanted to save Geordi. But I experienced something I did not expect —fear. I believe I should be deactivated until Dr. Crusher can remove the emotion chip."

"No," snapped Picard. "I need your full attention on this task."

Data continued to look miserable, and Picard sat down beside him. "Data, part of having emotions is learning how to deal with them. No matter what. You are an officer aboard this ship, and right now you have a duty to perform. Get a grip on yourself, Commander. That's an order."

Data stiffened his shoulders. "Yes, sir."

The computer beeped to signal that it was finished, and Data went back to work. "The destruction of the Amargosa star has had the following effects in this sector: Gamma emissions have increased by point-zero-five percent. The *Starship Bozeman* was forced to make a course correction—"

"Wait," said Picard. "Why did the *Bozeman* have to change course?"

"The destruction of the star altered the gravitational forces throughout the sector. Any ship passing through this region will have to make a minor course correction."

Picard looked excitedly at the readouts. "Could the

destruction of that star also change the course of the nexus?"

"Yes, sir," said Data with surprise. "I will plot its new course."

The captain added, "We know that any ship that gets too close to the nexus is destroyed. Soran can't fly *into* the nexus, so he has to make *it* come to *him!*"

The android's fingers danced across his console. "Yes," he agreed. "Dr. Soran would need a place to wait for the nexus, and he would probably choose a class-M planet. The Veridian system is in the path of the nexus, and it has two class-M planets."

"What would happen to the nexus if he destroyed the Veridian star?"

"The nexus would be diverted to Veridian Three, which is an uninhabited planet," answered Data. Then he looked worriedly at Picard. "But the other class-M planet has a population of over two hundred million people. They would all be destroyed by the shock wave."

The captain hit his comm badge. "Picard to bridge."

"Worf here," came the answer.

"Set a course for the Veridian system. Maximum warp." He and Data ran for the turbolift.

* * *

Lursa Duras sat impatiently in the command chair of the Klingon Bird of Prey. She would be glad to get rid of her passenger, Dr. Soran, but not until he gave them what they wanted. They needed that trilithium weapon. The Klingon Empire had grown soft from its alliance with the Federation. It needed new leadership —it needed her and B'Etor.

Her sister entered the bridge, followed by Dr. Soran.

"Did you get what you wanted from the human?" she asked.

"No," said Soran. "But I left him alive, for you to use as a hostage. Call it a going-away present."

The helmsman reported, "We are entering orbit around Veridian Three."

Soran clapped his hands and smiled. "Prepare to beam me to the surface."

"We want our payment," demanded B'Etor.

He handed her a small computer chip. "This contains all the information you'll need to build the weapon. It's been coded. Once I'm safely to the surface, I'll transmit the decryption code . . . but not before."

"Mistress!" barked the helmsman. "A Federation starship is entering the system!"

"What?" snarled Lursa. "On viewer."

64

She gasped when she saw the *Enterprise* come out of warp drive and go into orbit around the planet.

"They are hailing us," reported the helmsman. Like the other crew members, he looked frightened.

"On speakers."

Captain Picard's voice was loud and clear. "Klingon vessel, we know what you're doing. We will destroy any probe launched toward the Veridian star. We demand that you return our chief engineer and leave this system immediately."

Soran frowned and checked his pocket watch. "There is no time for this. Eliminate them."

B'Etor shook her head. "That is a Galaxy-class starship. We are no match for them."

Soran began to smile. "What if we knew all their secrets? Their weaknesses." He took Geordi's VISOR out of his pocket and gazed at it. "I think it's time we gave Mr. La Forge his sight back."

Several hundred kilometers away, Captain Picard was pacing on the bridge of the *Enterprise*. Riker, Data, and Worf looked on from their stations.

"They're trying to decide whether a twenty-year-old Klingon Bird of Prey is any match for the Federation flagship," said the captain.

Worf broke in. "Sir, a solar probe launched from either the Klingon ship or the planet's surface will

65

take eleven seconds to reach the sun. However, since we do not know the exact point of origin, it will take us between eight and fifteen seconds to lock our weapons on to it."

"So we're bluffing," said Riker. He looked grimly at Picard.

"How long until the nexus arrives?" asked Picard.

Data answered, "Approximately forty-seven minutes, sir."

"They are hailing us," said Worf.

"On screen."

The smiling but rugged faces of Lursa and B'Etor appeared on the main viewscreen.

"Captain," said Lursa. "What an unexpected pleasure."

Picard demanded, "Let me talk to Soran."

"I'm afraid the doctor is no longer aboard our ship," she answered.

"Then I'll beam down to his location," answered Picard. "Just give us his coordinates."

"The doctor values his privacy," said Lursa. "He would be quite upset if an armed party interrupted him."

"Then I can beam over to your ship," answered the captain. "And you can transport me to Soran."

Riker interrupted. "Sir, you can't trust them. For all

we know, they killed Geordi, and they'll kill you, too."

Lursa smiled, trying to look friendly. "We did not harm your engineer. He's been our guest. We would be happy to return him. And we will be happy to transport the captain."

Picard's lips thinned. He could see Riker about to protest, but it was *his* decision. His life for Geordi's. La Forge was a young man, in the prime of life, and Picard felt old. He had let his family down by not having any children. But he wouldn't fail his crew, or the two hundred million innocent people in this solar system.

"Number One," he said, "you have the bridge. Have Dr. Crusher meet me in Transporter Room Three."

"Aye, sir," muttered Riker.

With determination the captain strode toward the turbolift.

Moments later he stood on the transporter platform, waiting for the transporter chief to enter the coordinates. Beverly Crusher and Nurse Ogawa stood nearby, their medical equipment ready. Beverly gave him a brave smile, but he could tell she was worried. So was he, but he was determined to save as many lives as he could.

The transporter chief said, "Receiving coordinates, Captain."

Picard lifted his chin. "Energize."

The captain disappeared in a column of swirling lights at the same instant as Geordi appeared. The last thing he saw was Beverly and Ogawa rushing to help Geordi.

Then the captain was standing on a rugged mountaintop, surrounded by lush trees and bushes. He was surprised—the Duras sisters had actually kept their word. Of course, he told himself, they were staring at the *Enterprise,* which could blow them away in a matter of seconds. He noticed that his communication badge was gone.

In the distance Picard saw scaffolding that had been erected on a plateau. He followed a narrow ledge toward the platform, where a solar probe was waiting to be launched.

Also waiting there was Dr. Soran. He was calmly studying his pocket watch.

"Hello, Captain," he said. "You must think I'm quite the madman."

"The thought had crossed my mind," Picard answered.

"If you're here," said Soran, "then you're not sure you can shoot down my probe after all. So you've come to talk me out of my plan. Good luck."

Picard started toward Soran, but he struck an invisible forcefield which knocked him backward. He got to his feet and grabbed a handful of dirt, which he threw at the forcefield. The dirt crackled where it hit. It wasn't long before the captain discovered that the field completely surrounded the launch pad.

When Soran saw Picard's angry expression, he began to laugh.

Aboard the Klingon ship Lursa leaned over the shoulder of her navigator to get a better look at his instrument panel.

He grinned at her. "I have established a link with the camera we put inside the human's VISOR."

"Put it on screen," she ordered.

The viewscreen of the Klingon ship showed nothing but static for a few seconds. Then it cleared to show a ceiling on the *Enterprise*.

"It's working!" crowed Lursa.

Her sister was beside her. "Where is he?" asked B'Etor.

Suddenly Beverly Crusher's face and auburn hair loomed large on the viewscreen, as if she was leaning over Geordi. She smiled and talked to him. There wasn't any audio, but Lursa had a good idea where they were.

"That is sickbay," she said. She made a disgusted face. "Human females are so repulsive."

"When will he go to Engineering?" asked B'Etor.

Lursa stared at the screen. "We must be patient. Do not worry, my sister. We will get our opportunity to destroy the *Enterprise.*"

CHAPTER 8

Captain Picard walked all the way around the invisible forcefield, looking for a way to get in. He could see Soran, punching buttons on a remote-control device. The scientist moved to the launcher and adjusted the solar probe.

"Soran!" called the captain. "You don't need to do this. I'm sure we could find another way to get you into the nexus."

The El-Aurian shook his head. "Sorry, Captain. I've spent eighty years looking for another way, and this is the only one. Of course, you could always come with me. You fancy yourself an explorer. Here's a chance to explore something no human has ever experienced."

"No," said Picard. "Not if it means killing over two

hundred million people. I wonder . . . did your wife, Leandra, know that she married a mass murderer?"

Soran looked up angrily. For a moment Picard thought that he had struck some humanity inside the man. Then Soran gave him a smile.

"That's a nice try, Captain. But everyone I loved is dead. The nexus is the only way I can reach them now. If you would come with me, you would know."

Picard sighed and sat down on the ground. How could he stop him? He almost reached for his comm badge, then realized it was gone. On this mountaintop, it was just him and a madman. And he was the only one who could save two hundred million people.

On the Klingon Bird of Prey Lursa and B'Etor stared at their main viewscreen. They could see legs moving and soap suds floating on water. Geordi La Forge was taking a bath!

B'Etor growled, "He must be the only engineer in Starfleet who does not go to Engineering!"

"Our ship was too dirty for him," hissed Lursa. "But he suspects nothing. Let him get clean before he dies."

Commander Riker paced the bridge of the *Enterprise.* "Any luck, Mr. Worf?"

"No, sir, answered the security chief. "I am still unable to locate the captain. Our sensors can't penetrate the planet's ionosphere."

"Keep trying," said Riker worriedly. "Keep trying."

Captain Picard tossed pebbles at the forcefield, and they bounced off with little sparks. Soran continued to work on the launcher's control panel, making final adjustments. *There has to be some way to get in,* thought Picard. *There just had to be!*

He walked up to the forcefield and tried words again. "You know, Soran, what you're doing is no different from when the Borg destroyed your world."

"You're right," answered Soran, not looking up. "And there was a time when I wouldn't have hurt anyone. Then the Borg came. They showed me that if there is one constant in this universe, it's death."

Soran stood and brushed the dirt off his hands. "After the Borg came, I began to realize that none of it mattered. We're all going to die anyway. It's only a question of how and when. You'll die, too, Captain. You might contract a fatal disease. You might die in battle."

He looked at Picard with sharp blue eyes. "Or you might die in a fire."

Picard swallowed hard, trying not to think about his brother and his nephew. But Soran moved closer to him and stared at him across the forcefield.

"I've been to the nexus, Captain. I know things about people. Aren't you beginning to feel time gaining on you? It's like a predator. It's stalking you. You can try to outrun it with doctors, medicines, a new heart. But in the end time is going to hunt you down—and make the kill."

"We're all mortal," said Picard. "It's one of the truths of our existence."

Soran looked up at the sky, as if waiting for something. "I've found a new truth—the nexus. Time has no meaning there. The predator has no teeth."

Picard tried to think of something else to say. But what could he say to a man who was willing to kill millions of people for his own happiness?

After Soran went back to work, the captain started to walk around the forcefield again. Something on the ground suddenly caught his eye.

It was a large root from a nearby tree. The root poked out of the ground, leaving a small arch just big enough for a man to crawl under. The captain picked up some more pebbles and tossed them at the root. The ones that hit above the root bounced off the forcefield. The ones that hit below the root rolled through.

The forcefield did not extend *under* the root!

Soran looked back at him. "Careful, Captain. That's a fifty gigawatt forcefield. I wouldn't want to see you get hurt."

"Thank you," Picard answered. "I'm just killing time."

Soran chuckled. "No, Captain. Time is killing you."

Lursa bolted upright in her chair. She was still watching Geordi's movements through the camera hidden in his VISOR. It seemed as if it had taken hours for him to bathe and shave. But he was finally walking down a corridor—toward a door marked ENGINEERING.

"B'Etor!" she screamed.

Her sister bounced out of her chair and stared at the screen. "Are we recording this?"

"Yes, Mistress," answered a crewman.

Lursa held her breath as Geordi walked into Engineering. His staff greeted him with smiles and happy faces. Then the viewpoint shifted around to all the consoles and instrument panels as Geordi checked them.

Lursa knew that Soran was crazy, but he was also brilliant. She would never have thought of anything as devious as this.

Another engineer took Geordi aside and showed him a large cutaway diagram of the *Enterprise*. They saw everything—weapon systems, plasma relays, generator, warp coil, defensive shields. It was like getting a guided tour!

"That's it!" she barked. "Replay the diagram of the shields."

B'Etor rushed to a console and rewound the image.

"Magnify that section and enhance," said Lursa.

B'Etor worked swiftly, and the image grew larger until they could see blocks of numbers and text.

Lursa howled with laughter. "Their shields are operating on a modulation of two-five-seven-point-four!"

B'Etor grinned and turned to the weapons officer. "Adjust our torpedo frequency to match it."

"Yes, Mistress," he said eagerly.

B'Etor slapped her hands together. "Fire when ready!"

The *Enterprise* was rocked by a terrific explosion. Alarms went off on the bridge, and red lights began to flash. Most of the crew members were knocked off their feet, and some stayed down.

Worf staggered back to his post. In shock he reported, "They are firing torpedoes. Our shields have no effect!"

"Lock phasers and return fire!" shouted Riker.

Another direct hit threw everyone to the floor. Instrument panels began to explode. Smoke and sparks filled the air.

Riker stood up and wiped blood off his forehead. "Damage report!"

Data was nearly screaming with terror as he reported, "All systems failing! Hull breach on decks thirty-one through thirty-five. Shields ineffective!"

Another blast jolted them, and the lights began to dim.

Riker rushed to Worf's side. "That's an old Klingon ship. What do we know about it? Are there any weaknesses?"

"It is a class-D-twelve Bird of Prey," answered the Klingon. "They were retired from service because of defective plasma coils."

Riker stared at the viewscreen. The Klingon ship was old, but it had plenty of torpedoes. He turned to see a crewman lying dead on the floor beside him.

"Plasma coils?" said Riker desperately. "Can we can use that to our advantage?"

Worf shook his head. "I do not see how. The plasma coil is part of their cloaking device—"

Riker shouted above the alarms, "Data! Can we disrupt their plasma coil with some kind of ionic pulse?"

The android cocked his head to consider the question. "Yes!" he chirped. "A low-level ionic pulse might reset the coil and trigger their cloaking device. Excellent idea, sir!"

Worf grinned. "As their cloak begins to engage, their shields will drop."

"And they'll be vulnerable for at least two seconds," said Riker. "Data, lock on to that plasma coil."

The android grinned. "No problem." He ran to a bulkhead, ripped open a panel, and began pulling out circuits.

Riker turned to Worf. "Prepare a spread of photon torpedoes. We're only going to get one shot at this. Target their primary reactor."

"Aye, sir." The Klingon readied his weapons.

On the Bird of Prey Lursa rubbed her hands together and grinned. She could smell victory! Once it was known that the Duras sisters had destroyed the *Enterprise,* the Klingon Empire would be at their feet.

"Our shields are holding against their phasers," said B'Etor with satisfaction.

"Target their bridge," Lursa ordered. "Let's put them out of their misery."

The navigator made a sudden grunt. "Mistress! We are cloaking!"

"What!" screamed B'Etor.

"Our shields are down!" he shouted.

"Evasive action!" yelled Lursa.

But it was too late. She turned to the viewscreen to see the crippled *Enterprise* unleash a spread of photon torpedoes. She didn't even have time to cover her eyes before they hit their target.

From the *Enterprise* they watched the Klingon ship explode in a brilliant white light. Gases and pieces of metal erupted toward them, and the Bird of Prey was no more. There was nothing left but bits of junk, floating in space.

"Yes!" screamed Data, stabbing his fist in the air.

Riker smiled and patted Worf on the back. "Well done, all of you. Let's get some repair crews working. And medical crews. We'd better plan to dock for repairs. Data, what's the nearest starbase?"

Before Data could answer, Geordi's voice broke over the comm link. "La Forge to bridge! We're about five minutes from a warp core breach! There's nothing I can do."

Riker rushed to the command chair. A warp core breach meant only one thing—the *Enterprise* was five minutes away from destruction!

CHAPTER

Commander Troi's voice rang out over the entire ship. "Emergency evacuation! Everyone into the saucer section! We are preparing to separate the ship. This is *not* a drill!"

A special alarm sounded, and Dr. Crusher dropped her medical kit. For seven years they had practiced separating the saucer section from the hull, which contained the warp engines. Now it was for real!

She picked up a wounded woman and dragged her to the door of sickbay. She saw Nurse Ogawa trying to unfold a stretcher.

"Ogawa!" she yelled. "Make the wounded walk! There won't be room in the corridor for stretchers. Just get them out of here! Every second counts!"

In the corridor schoolchildren rushed out of a classroom and ran toward the turbolift. One teacher guided them, and the other counted them as they ran. The corridor was choked with people, but there was no panic. They all knew this day might come.

A little girl had her arms full of toys, and her mother took them away from her. "No belongings!" she warned.

Seeing the girl's sad expression, the mother handed her back her teddy bear. But she tossed the other toys into their quarters, and the doors snapped shut on them.

Suddenly Beverly saw Deanna Troi. She was carrying a child under each arm. "Come on, let's go!" she yelled at the adults. "Grab the children! And the wounded!"

The adults threw away whatever they were carrying and grabbed those who could not run for themselves. A panel door suddenly banged open, and Worf stood there on a metal ladder.

"This way!" he yelled in his booming voice. "The turbolifts are too crowded!"

Dozens of adults lined up and began to follow him up the ladder. Beverly was frightened, but she was proud of the crew of the *Enterprise*. Civilians, children—they all knew what they had to do. If they didn't reach the saucer section, they would die when the warp coil blew.

On the mountaintop of Veridian Three, it was peaceful. A cool breeze was blowing, and the trees rustled softly. Soran was sitting on a rock, looking at his pocket watch. He occasionally glanced at Picard.

The captain was waiting. He knew what he had to do—crawl under that root—but he couldn't do it with Soran watching him. He could see a disruptor weapon on Soran's belt, and he knew the madman would use it. The captain had to wait until the scientist was distracted.

Soran slapped his hand on his knees and stood up. He checked the launcher one last time. Then he nodded with satisfaction.

"Thank you for waiting with me, Captain," he said. "If you'll excuse me, I have an appointment with eternity. And I don't want to be late."

Soran began to climb up the scaffolding toward the top of the rockface. Picard watched him intently for a few moments, then dashed toward the root. He dropped to the ground and started to wriggle underneath the root. It was a tight fit, and there wasn't much room.

Suddenly his shoulder hit the forcefield, and the energy crackled all around him.

On the scaffolding Soran whirled around at the sound. Angrily he drew the disruptor and fired! The ground around Picard was blasted apart, creating a huge cloud of dirt and smoke.

Soran moved to the edge of the scaffolding to get a better look. He couldn't tell if he had killed Picard or not, but he was ready to shoot him again. When the dust from the explosion finally cleared, there was nothing but a hole in the ground.

"Picard!" he yelled. "Where are you?"

There was no answer, but the wind began to pick up. Soran looked up in the sky to see something in the distance—the energy ribbon!

The nexus was coming! Coming for *him!*

"One minute to warp core breach," said Data. He couldn't hide the fear in his voice.

Commander Riker drummed his fingers on the arm of his chair. He had to wait. But how long?

Suddenly Geordi's breathless voice cut in. "That's it, bridge. We're all in the saucer!"

Riker nodded and looked at Data. "Begin separation sequence." He turned to Deanna Troi, who was manning the helm. "Full impulse power once we're clear."

"Yes, sir," she answered.

Data set to work, and the viewscreen showed a

simulation of what was happening to the *Enterprise*. Slowly a crack began to form between the flat saucer section and the hull. The sweeping nacelles were part of the hull, and they fired briefly to help the separation. With a shudder the saucer pulled free.

"Separation complete," said Data. "Ten seconds to warp core breach."

"Engaging impulse engines," Deanna announced.

Riker balled his hands into fists. Had they given themselves enough time? A moment later the ship was rocked by a terrible explosion as the hull blew apart behind them. Everyone was knocked to the floor.

"Report," snapped Riker.

"Helm is not responding!" said Deanna.

They looked up at the viewscreen to see the planet of Veridian Three rushing toward them.

"Uh-oh," said Data.

The ship began shaking violently. In the lower decks of the saucer section, children screamed and hung on to their parents. The little girl hugged her teddy bear as objects flew through the air and crashed to the deck. They all held their breath.

Riker stared wide-eyed at the viewscreen. The planet filled the entire screen. He could see forests, seas, and mountains—rushing toward them.

Data's fingers flew over his console. "I have rerouted auxiliary power to the lateral thrusters. Attempting to level our descent."

Riker pressed the comm panel and announced, "All hands brace for impact!"

At the last moment the nose of the gigantic saucer tilted upward, just before it smashed into the ground. The saucer ripped a path through the forest as wide as a spacedock. Trees were thrown aside like toothpicks, and hills were turned into dust. Nothing stood in its way.

The crew on the bridge were thrown violently against the deck and bulkheads. Deanna started to fly into the viewscreen, but Data grabbed her at the last second. Every instrument panel exploded at once, showering them with sparks and smoke. The ship's lights went out, plunging them into darkness.

The terror seemed to go on forever, and then it suddenly stopped. There was a crash, and the lights came back on. Riker shielded his eyes and looked up at the ceiling. He blinked in amazement.

It wasn't the ship's lights that were on. There was a giant hole in the top of the bridge, and sunlight was streaming through. Two strange-looking birds landed on the rim of the open hole and looked down at him.

He laughed with relief.

* * *

On another part of the planet Dr. Soran was climbing up the scaffolding. Suddenly a boot kicked him in the face, and he went sprawling backward. Picard had made it inside the forcefield!

The captain jumped on Soran and fought with the only weapons he had—his fists. They rolled over the top of the scaffolding, and Soran tried to draw his disruptor. But Picard knocked the weapon out of his hand, and it fell harmlessly into the dirt.

Ferociously the El-Aurian fought back. He was strong and determined, and he struck Picard with a series of blows. The captain tumbled off the scaffolding and fell onto the lower level. He shook his head and looked up. That was when he saw it.

A vast energy ribbon sparkled across the sky like the northern lights. It was the nexus, getting closer. His time was almost up.

Picard rolled away as Soran's boot just missed his head. He struggled to his feet and smashed the scientist in the face. There was no more time to fight—he had to disable the probe before it launched!

Picard climbed toward the launcher, straining with every muscle in his body. Suddenly the launcher roared, and smoke poured over him. He shielded his eyes and stared after the probe as it vanished into the sky.

The captain dropped down off the ladder. He

prayed the *Enterprise* would shoot down the probe, but it didn't. He watched helplessly as a dark spot appeared on the Veridian sun. Slowly the entire sun darkened, just like the Amargosa sun had. It was collapsing! Picard slumped onto the ground and pounded it with his fists.

He had failed.

Soran howled with triumph and climbed to the top of the scaffolding. He stood there, his arms outstretched, as the giant ribbon of energy rushed toward them.

A fierce wind began to whip the mountain plateau, and Picard shivered with the cold. The only light in the darkened sky was the nexus, and it was getting larger. The captain struggled to his feet, but there was nowhere to run. The shimmering lights of the nexus seemed to swallow the entire sky.

Then it swallowed Picard and Soran, and the mountaintop. A second later the shock wave hit, and the planet exploded in a blaze of flame.

And everything was gone.

CHAPTER
10

Captain Picard found himself walking down a long hallway. He couldn't tell where he was, because he was wearing a blindfold. Small hands were leading him, and he heard giggling.

Then he was in a large room. He heard a crackling sound, and he could feel the warmth of the fire in the fireplace. There was a fresh, outdoorsy smell about the place. The hands released him, and he stood there, wondering what to do next.

"What's going on?" he asked. "Where am I?"

Hands reached up and pulled off the blindfold. He blinked his eyes as the blurry colors came into focus. The first thing he saw was an enormous Christmas tree. It was blazing with hundreds of sparkling lights and decorations, and there was an angel sitting on the top.

Picard looked around the living room of his home in France. He didn't know how he knew it was his living room, but it was. It was exactly the way he would want his living room to look on Christmas, with holly draped over the windows and presents piled under the tree.

Then his eyes focused on the people in the room. At the sight of his lovely wife and his five beautiful children, he grinned like a fool. He felt like crying with joy.

Olivia, Thomas, Madison, Matthew, and little Mimi—he knew all their names. Of course he did, they were his children! The boys even looked like him.

His wife smiled. "Go on . . . say something. They're waiting."

He shook his head. "I don't know what to say."

Olivia, his eldest daughter, spoke up. "Say Merry Christmas, Papa!"

"Merry Christmas!" he replied joyfully.

The children broke into applause, and the woman rushed forward to kiss him. She smelled so wonderful. They led him to his favorite easy chair, and the children began to hand out the presents.

"Where's my present for Papa?" asked Madison, rooting through the pile.

Matthew found one for himself. "I hope this is the book I asked for. *The Fabulist.*"

"This one's for Papa," said Olivia with a big smile.

"You open yours first," Picard told them all. "I have plenty of time."

As the activity swirled around him, Picard sat back in his easy chair. He had never felt such happiness and contentment. He never wanted this day to end.

"Isn't the tree beautiful, Papa?" asked little Mimi.

"Oh, yes," he said with a smile. "It's astonishingly beautiful. All of it."

Matthew, his youngest son, pushed a present into his lap. "This is from all of us," he said.

They waited, smiling. Picard knew this was what they had been whispering about for weeks. "Thank you," he said. "I can't imagine what it is."

He ripped open the box as eagerly as any child. He gasped when he saw what was inside. It was a nineteenth-century sextant. The ancient navigational instrument was made of gleaming brass.

Thomas blurted out, "It's a sack-tent!"

Now the tears were flowing from his eyes. "Where on Earth did you find it?"

"It's a secret," said Mimi.

"That makes it doubly special. Thank you. Thank you all." He enveloped the children in one giant hug.

"We love you, Papa!" Mimi shouted.

And they did. Picard felt their love sweeping over him. It was the most glorious feeling he had ever had.

His wife was beaming with pride. "If I know this crew, they'll be hungry soon. I'd best get dinner started."

A minute later the children were busy with new toys, new books, and new games. Picard took a moment to stretch his legs and look more closely at the Christmas tree. He could remember most of the ornaments from Christmases past. But there was one ornament in particular he wanted to see more closely.

It was a beautiful glass ball with a tiny light in the center. The light was in the shape of a star, and it blinked on and off. The ornament reminded him of something, but he couldn't think what. It was something troubling, something he didn't want to think about.

He turned to look out the window, at the swirling snowflakes outside. In the reflection in the window, he could still see the glass ball. The star inside it kept blinking on and off. On and off.

Picard rubbed his eyes. "This isn't right," he muttered. "This can't be real."

"It's as real as you want it to be," said a familiar voice.

The captain turned to see Guinan. The children kept playing, ignoring them.

"What's going on?" he asked. "Where am I?"

"You're in the nexus."

He looked around at the beautiful living room. "Is this what it's like?"

"For you. This is where you wanted to be."

He shook his head. "But I never had a wife, children, a home like this."

Guinan gave him a strange smile. "Enjoy them, Jean-Luc. They're all for you."

"What are you doing here?" he asked. "I thought you were on the *Enterprise.*"

"I am on the *Enterprise,*" she replied. "I am also here. Think of me as an echo of the person you know. A part of me that was left behind when the *Enterprise*-B beamed us off."

"Soran, too?" asked Picard. His fight with Soran, the star collapsing—it was coming back to him now.

"All of us," she answered. "Now do you see why he wanted to return so badly?"

"Where is he now?"

Guinan shrugged. "Wherever he wants to be."

"Papa!" yelled Thomas. "Help me build my castle."

Picard looked over at the boy. He had a set of interlocking blocks that were supposed to form a castle. *But that castle isn't any more real than this living room,* thought Picard.

"In a few minutes," said the captain. He knew that

if he helped build that castle, he might stay in this place forever. Forever happy and content.

"You've got great kids," said Guinan. "You can go back and see them born. Or go forward and see your grandchildren. Time has no meaning here."

"Dinner is almost ready!" called his wife from the kitchen.

Matthew grabbed his hand. "Come on, Papa! It's your favorite!"

That is certain, thought Picard. Whatever he did here, it would be his favorite. He looked at the boy and his other children. They were so wonderful, more than any father could hope for. But what about the millions of children who died when the Veridian sun exploded? They were *real* children.

"Go on," he said finally. "Go on without me."

The boy gave him a funny look, but he would never disobey his father. Soon all the children were gone, and Picard was alone with Guinan. The living room suddenly felt colder.

"Can I leave the nexus?" he asked her.

"Why would you want to leave?"

"Just tell me if I can."

She nodded. "I told you—time has no meaning here. If you leave, you can go anywhere. Anyplace in time."

Picard took a deep breath. "I know exactly where I

want to go. Back to that mountaintop on Veridian Three. Before Soran destroyed their star. I have to stop him."

"You failed to stop him before," said Guinan. "Why would it be different the next time?"

"You're right," answered Picard. "I'll need help. You can come with me, and together—"

"No," she said. "I'm just an echo of someone who is already there."

Picard frowned. He was defeated before he started.

Guinan looked thoughtful. "But I know just the guy."

In a flash the scenery changed, and Picard found himself standing outdoors. He heard the cry of a hawk, and he looked up to see the bird circling above him. The view was spectacular—mountains, clear blue sky, a beautiful meadow with a trace of snow on the ground. He could plainly see his breath in the chill air.

Picard looked around for Guinan, but she was gone. Then he saw a two-story farmhouse in the distance. It was rustic but substantial, well built. *This has to be somebody's dream,* he thought. *But whose?*

He heard an ax chopping wood, and he followed the sound to the house. Rounding a corner, he saw a husky older man. He was chopping wood, working hard, and there was sweat on his brow. He was also wearing a Starfleet uniform.

Captain James T. Kirk! Picard recognized him from his portrait at Starfleet Academy. But he was dead, wasn't he? Then he remembered that Kirk had died on the mission that had taken Guinan, Soran, and the others from the nexus. Kirk was alive, and he was chopping wood as if it was his favorite thing in the whole world to do.

Picard's footsteps crunched on the snow, and Kirk looked up. "Beautiful day, isn't it?"

"Yes," agreed Picard. "Yes, it is." He doubted if there were many terrible days inside the nexus.

Kirk pointed to a nearby log. "Do you mind?"

Picard realized that Kirk wanted him to put the log on the chopping block. He obliged, and the captain split it with one forceful swing.

The younger captain swallowed, wondering how to broach the subject of the nexus. How much did Kirk know about his existence here?

"Captain Kirk," he said, "do you realize what—"

But Kirk held up his hand and sniffed the air. "Wait a second. I think something's burning."

Kirk dashed toward the house, and Picard turned to see smoke billowing out of one of the windows.

He followed Kirk through the back door of the

house, which opened into a lovely kitchen. The house was decorated with Early American furnishings, and the kitchen was warm and friendly. Among the many appliances were an antique oven and a computer-controlled bread-maker. There was a Starfleet plaque stuck on the refrigerator.

Kirk hurried to the stove and pulled a smoking frying pan off the fire. It was hot, and he nearly threw it into the sink. As he ran the water and brushed the smoke away, he saw that Picard had followed him in.

"Looks as if somebody was cooking eggs," said Kirk, wrinkling his nose. "Come on in, it's all right. This is my house—or at least it used to be. I sold it years ago."

Picard decided that he had to use the direct approach. "I'm Captain Jean-Luc Picard of the *Starship Enterprise.*"

Before Kirk could answer, an antique clock on the windowsill chimed three bells. The captain gazed at it fondly. "I gave that clock to Bones," he said, "I don't know how many years ago."

Picard plowed ahead. "I'm not from your *Enterprise.* I'm from what you would consider the future— the twenty-fourth century."

They heard a bark, and a big, rangy dog bounded into the kitchen. Kirk bent down to pet him, and the dog eagerly licked his face.

"Jake!" he exclaimed. "You miserable old mutt! You're looking good, considering you've been dead seven years."

A woman's voice called from somewhere upstairs, "Jim! I'm starving. How long are you going to be rattling around in that kitchen?"

Kirk shook his head in amazement. "That's Antonia's voice."

He turned to stare at Picard. "How can you be from the future? What are you talking about? This is the *past.*"

Then Kirk rushed to a drawer and yanked it open. Slowly he removed an old horseshoe with a tiny red bow tied around it. He smiled with relief, as if he finally knew where he was.

"This is nine years ago," said Kirk. "It's the day I told her I was going back to Starfleet."

The old captain touched his head, as if the memories were giving him a headache. He went back to the frying pan in the sink and stared at the soggy eggs.

"Those were Ktarian eggs," said Kirk with realization. "I was cooking them to soften the blow." He held up the horseshoe. "And I gave this to her to hang over the door. She was always a little superstitious."

With sympathy Picard told him, "I know how real this must seem to you. But it's not real. This isn't your house, or your kitchen. We've both been caught up in some sort of temporal nexus."

Kirk snapped his fingers. "Dillweed."

As Picard looked on with despair, Kirk dumped the ruined eggs into the sink and took the frying pan back to the stove. He went to the pantry and grabbed two fresh eggs, which he promptly cracked into the pan.

"This time I've got a chance to do it right," he said excitedly. "There's a bottle of dillweed on the second shelf to the left, right behind the nutmeg."

Picard searched for the spice and handed it to him. "How long have you been here?" he asked.

Kirk shrugged. "I don't know. I was on the *Enterprise*-B, trying to save the ship by adjusting the deflector relays. And the bulkhead in front of me just disappeared! Then I was out there, chopping wood."

"According to our history," said Picard, "you died saving the *Enterprise*-B almost eighty years ago."

Kirk laughed as he cooked his eggs. "So you're telling me this is the twenty-fourth century, and I'm dead? I don't feel dead. I feel alive for the first time in years!"

"You're not dead," said Picard, getting desperate. "As I said, this is some kind of temporal nexus, and we—"

Kirk scowled. "Yeah, I heard you." He scooped the

eggs off the skillet and put them on a plate. Then he set the plate on a tray, along with a cloth napkin, a glass of orange juice, and a small vase of flowers.

"Let me see," said Kirk, puzzled. "Something's missing?"

At his question two slices of toast popped out of the toaster. With a smile Kirk grabbed them and set them on the plate. Then he picked up the tray and headed out the swinging door.

Picard caught up with him as he was climbing an old-fashioned staircase, tray in hand.

"Captain!" he called. "I need your help. I want you to leave the nexus with me. We have to go back to a planet called Veridian Three—to stop a man from destroying a star! There are millions of lives at stake."

Kirk smiled. "I'm dead, remember. Who am I to argue with history?"

"You're a Starfleet officer, and you have a duty to—"

Kirk cut him off. "I don't need to be lectured by *you*. I was out saving the galaxy when your grandfather was still in diapers! And frankly, I think the galaxy owes me one."

The old captain frowned with a painful memory. "I was like you once—worried about duty all the time. What did it get me? An empty house. Not this time!

I'm going to walk up these stairs, march into that bedroom, and tell Antonia that I want to marry her."

Kirk did exactly that, and he slammed the door in Picard's face.

In frustration Picard rushed after Kirk and flung open the bedroom door . . .

Only to find himself standing inside a wooden barn! Sunlight was streaming through the old wooden slats. There were stalls full of horses, and the air smelled of fresh-cut hay and alfalfa. A fly buzzed around his ear.

Captain Kirk stood in the center of the barn, looking around in amazement. His tray of food was gone.

"This doesn't look like your bedroom," remarked Picard.

"No. No, it's not," answered Kirk. "It's better! This is my uncle's barn in Iowa."

He rushed to a stall and rubbed the nose of a big strawberry roan horse. "I took this horse out for a ride seven years ago. On a beautiful spring day just like this one. If I'm right, this is the day I met Antonia!"

Kirk grinned at Picard. "This nexus of yours is very clever. I can start all over again—do things right from day one."

Kirk flung open the stall door, grabbed the reins, and led the horse out. The roan was already saddled and stomping the ground, eager to run. Kirk leaped upon his back like a joyful teenager. With a wild holler he galloped out the door of the barn and was gone.

Picard grimaced in anger and searched the stalls for another saddled horse. When he found a gray horse with some Arabian blood in her, he led her out of the stall. Picard preferred an English saddle, but the Western saddle would have to do. He mounted and rode in pursuit of Captain Kirk.

He could see Kirk and his red horse in the distance, pounding hard across the countryside. The roan splashed through a stream and ducked between a thicket of trees. Picard gamely followed.

Then Picard saw something that caused him to pull up his horse sharply. Kirk was riding at full clip toward a deep ravine. There was no time for him to stop—he was going to try to jump it! Picard kicked his horse to catch up.

Like a runaway freight train, Kirk and the roan bore down on the ravine. Picard nearly averted his eyes, but then he remembered where he was. He watched calmly as Kirk and the big roan took the ravine with a flying leap. For good measure they wheeled around and leaped over again, to come back where they started.

Picard slowed his gray to a trot and caught up with the captain, who was hardly winded by his derring-do.

Kirk pointed toward the ravine. "I must have made

that jump fifty times, and every time it scared the hell out of me. But not this time." He shook his head. "Because it's not real."

Kirk gazed off into the distance, and Picard followed his gaze to see a woman. She was walking her palomino horse, shielding her eyes from the bright sun with her hand. And she was headed toward them.

"Antonia?" asked Picard.

Kirk muttered, "She's not real, either, is she? Nothing here is real, so nothing matters." The old captain's shoulders slumped. "It's kind of like orbital skydiving. It's exciting for a few minutes, but in the end you haven't really done anything. You haven't made a difference."

Kirk looked at Picard as if he was seeing him for the first time. "Captain of the *Enterprise,* huh?"

"That's right. The *Enterprise*-D."

Kirk looked bitter for a moment. "Don't ever retire! Don't let them promote you to some desk job. You stay on the bridge of that ship, because while you're there, you can make a difference."

"Come with me," said Picard. "You don't have to be on the bridge of a starship to make a difference. Help me stop Soran. Make a difference right now."

Kirk grinned. "How can I argue with the captain of the *Enterprise?* What's the name of that planet? Veridian Three?"

Picard nodded. "That's right."

"I take it the odds are against us. The situation is grim?"

"You could say that," answered Picard. "Millions of lives are at stake."

Kirk rubbed his chin. "Of course, if Spock were here, he'd say I was being an irrational, illogical human for wanting to go on a mission like that."

He slapped Picard on the back. "But it sounds like fun!"

CHAPTER 11

Captain Picard was again standing on a mountaintop on Veridian Three. Dr. Soran walked toward the launchpad of the probe.

"Thank you for waiting with me, Captain," he said. "If you'll excuse me, I have an appointment with eternity. And I don't want to be late."

Soran began to climb up the scaffolding toward the top of the rockface. Picard watched him intently for a few moments, then he dashed toward the root. He dropped to the ground and started to wriggle underneath the root. It was a tight fit, and there wasn't much room.

Suddenly his shoulder hit the forcefield, and the energy crackled all around him.

On the scaffolding Soran whirled around at the sound. Angrily he drew the disruptor and fired! The ground around Picard was blasted apart, creating a huge cloud of dirt and smoke.

Soran moved to the edge of the scaffolding to get a better look. He couldn't tell if he had killed Picard or not, but he was ready to shoot him again.

Before he could get off another shot, a pair of boots kicked him in the back. The disruptor was knocked out of his hands.

Soran whirled around to see Captain James T. Kirk. Kirk swung his fist at him but missed, and Soran caught him with a punch to the stomach. The captain staggered against the scaffolding, and Soran hit him with several more brutal punches.

Picard didn't have time to worry about either one of them. He picked himself off the ground and climbed the ladder to the probe launcher. Soran saw what he was doing and started to come after him, but Kirk caught him from behind and threw him on the ground.

The shimmering nexus grew larger in the sky.

Picard ripped open the control panel of the launcher. It was full of strange screens with alien lettering. Some of it looked like numbers that were counting down. Picard hit several buttons—with no effect.

He looked over his shoulder and saw Soran and Kirk rolling on the ground. They were both struggling to get to the disruptor weapon.

Picard tried another button, and the screen abruptly changed to a picture of the Veridian sun. He could see the crosshairs that aimed that probe. He pressed another button . . .

And the probe disappeared!

A cloaking device, thought Picard. What would he do now?

Then he remembered that Soran had been using a remote-control device. He turned his attention back to the struggle on the ground. With a last-ditch effort Kirk staggered to his feet and smashed Soran in the mouth. The scientist sprawled to the ground and looked dazed. Captain Kirk gripped his back, obviously in pain.

"Kirk!" yelled Picard. "There's a control device in his right pocket!"

Grimacing in pain, the captain bent down and began searching Soran's pockets. He finally got the control device and began pressing buttons. While he did that, Soran shook his head and sat up.

The disruptor was just out of his reach, and Soran lunged for it. Kirk was too busy to notice.

Picard was going to warn him, but the probe was suddenly visible again. He found a small trackball, and he began to move the crosshairs away from the target.

"Hey!" yelled Kirk with a smile. "The twenty-fourth century isn't so tough."

Soran shot him in the back with the disruptor, and Kirk pitched forward.

The next instant the launcher roared to life, and Picard barely had time to jump off. He shielded his eyes as the probe soared into the sky.

Soran threw away the disruptor and began to cheer. But the probe made a sweeping turn and arced back toward the planet. Picard heard a muffled explosion and saw a plume of smoke in the distant jungle.

"No!" screamed Soran. The nexus filled the sky, but it wasn't coming any closer. Soran scrambled to the top of the scaffolding and held his arms out, trying to reach it. The ribbon of colors came close to his fingertips, but not quite. The doorway through time finally moved away and disappeared.

Picard jumped down and hurried to help Captain Kirk. He was still alive, but he was breathing heavily. Picard could see he was badly wounded.

"You!" screamed Soran at the top of his lungs. He shook his fists at Picard, then ran to leap off the scaffolding.

Picard was one step faster. He grabbed the disruptor just as Soran sailed through the air. The blast caught Soran in the chest, and he crumpled to the ground, dead. His pocket watch lay smashed beside him.

Picard rushed back to Captain Kirk and cradled his head in his arms.

"Nice shot," rasped Kirk. He coughed, and his eyelids fluttered.

"Try to hang on," said Picard. "I'll find a way to contact the *Enterprise.*"

Kirk didn't seem to hear him. "Did we do it? Did we make a difference?"

"Yes," whispered Picard. "Thank you."

"Least I could do . . . for a captain of the *Enterprise.*" Kirk coughed, and his breathing sounded worse.

"You'll be all right," said Picard. But they both knew he was lying.

Kirk looked up in the sky at the warm sun. He smiled and seemed to be at peace. "It was fun," he said.

Captain James T. Kirk had cheated death so many times. But not this time. He died in Captain Picard's arms.

It was late afternoon by the time Picard laid the last rock on Captain Kirk's grave. He took Kirk's old-fashioned insignia pin from his pocket and set it between the rocks.

He heard the distant whine of engines, and he looked up to see a shuttlecraft flying toward him. With a weary smile Picard waved to them.

They landed a moment later, and the captain was disturbed to see that the shuttlecraft was quite banged up. Not only that, but Geordi had a bandage on his face, and Worf's uniform was ripped and dirty. *Of course,* thought Picard, *I don't look much better.*

"Captain!" called Geordi as he stepped off the craft. "Are you all right?"

"I was about to ask you the same question."

Worf scowled. "The Duras sisters attacked the *Enterprise.* We destroyed them, but we had to make an emergency saucer separation."

"The hull section?" asked Picard.

Worf shook his head. "Gone."

"We've contacted Starfleet," said Geordi, "and they're sending the *Farragut* to pick us up."

Picard was still in shock. "You mean, the *Enterprise* is really finished?"

Geordi nodded sadly.

"Come," said Picard, "I want to see what's left of my ship."

"What about Dr. Soran?" asked Geordi.

Picard shook his head. "You needn't worry about the doctor anymore."

Deanna Troi tried to wipe the grease, dirt, and blood off her hands, but the stains seemed to be permanently ingrained. Her shiny black hair felt like a rat's nest. *Ah, well,* she thought, soon she could look forward to a hot bath aboard the *Farragut.*

The counselor glanced around at the pathetic wreckage of the *Enterprise.* There wasn't enough left of her to sell to a Ferengi junkyard. The hull had been blown to pieces, which were scattered through space. The saucer section was nothing but twisted metal and scorched circuits.

But there were plenty of people to be saved. Deanna had been helping to carry the wounded outside to be transported. Now she staggered back into sickbay, with Nurse Ogawa right behind her.

Ogawa wiped the sweat off her brow. "That should be the last of the wounded, Doctor."

Beverly Crusher nodded wearily, as if she was too tired to speak. She looked gaunt, her lovely cheekbones prominent.

"Two hundred and thirty-two patients in two days," she groaned.

Ogawa bent down to pick up a stretcher.

"Save that stretcher," said Beverly.

"Is there another patient?" asked the nurse.

Beverly smiled wanly. "No, that one's for *me.*"

From the corner of her eye Deanna saw Data walking through the corridor outside sickbay. He was carrying a tricorder and looked very serious.

"Do you need me anymore?" asked the counselor.

Beverly shook her head and tried to smile. "Go ahead. Thanks."

Deanna quickly caught up with the android and followed a few steps behind him. He was scanning the wreckage with his tricorder as he walked. She couldn't imagine why, because all the crew were accounted for.

He turned to look at her. "Are you busy, Counselor?"

"No," she admitted. "What's the matter?"

"Personal business," said the android glumly. "Spot is still missing."

"Oh, no! Get me another tricorder, and I'll help you look for her."

Ten minutes later they were on a cargo deck, sifting through the rubble for lifesigns. Deanna was afraid they wouldn't find Spot, and she wondered what it would do to Data's already overloaded emotions.

More to make conversation than anything else, she asked, "How are you feeling?"

Data cocked his head. "It has been difficult, but I believe I have the situation under control."

"So you've decided not to remove the emotion chip?"

"For now," he answered. "At first I was not prepared for the unpredictable nature of emotions. But after experiencing two hundred sixty-one distinct emotional states, I believe I have learned to control my feelings. They will no longer control me."

"Well, Data, I hope that you—" She was interrupted by a beep on her tricorder.

It was a lifesign!

Data peered over her shoulder and followed the indicator to an area of the cargo bay where several heavy-duty shelves had collapsed. With his tremendous strength the android pulled plates of metal aside as if they were cardboard.

Now Deanna peered over his shoulder, holding her breath. As the last metal sheet was removed, she heard a plaintive "Meow." Data reached down and gently lifted his orange cat, now nearly black.

"Spot!" He sighed with relief. He cradled the cat to his chest, and she purred with pleasure. "I am very happy to find you, Spot."

Deanna grinned. "Another family reunited."

With surprise Data put a finger to his eye and held the finger out to look at it. It was glistening wet.

"Data, are you all right?" asked Deanna.

The android shook his head. "I am not sure,

Counselor. I am happy to see Spot, yet I am crying. Am I still malfunctioning?"

"No, Data," she answered. "I think you're functioning perfectly."

In time-honored tradition Captain Picard and Commander Riker were the last of the *Enterprise* crew to leave the fallen ship. While the *Farragut* waited for them to beam up, the captain searched through the rubble of his ready room. He doubted if there was anything worth saving, but he wanted to take a final look, anyway.

Picard felt terrible about losing the *Enterprise,* but he couldn't help feeling good about himself. He had renewed energy, a renewed sense of purpose. Reality wasn't always pleasant, but you couldn't make a difference if you lived in a fantasy world.

Commander Riker poked his head through the jagged hole that had once been a doorway. "Still can't find it, sir?"

The captain stiffened his back and shook his head. "It doesn't matter, Number One."

"It's all this dust," said Riker. He grabbed a plaque that had fallen off the wall and waved it like a fan. After a cloud of dust spewed into the air, the bearded officer bent down to pick up a photo album.

"Is this it?" he asked, handing the album to Picard.

The captain beamed with pleasure and clutched the book. It was the album that contained his family photos of Robert and René. "Yes, Will. Thank you."

Riker stepped back into the bridge area and stared sadly at the toppled chairs and blackened instrument panels.

"I'm going to miss this ship," he said. "She went before her time."

Picard looked at the younger man. "It's not how many years you've lived, but how you've lived them. Someone once told me that time is a predator that stalks us all our lives. But maybe time is also a companion. It goes with us on our journey and reminds us to cherish the moments of our lives. Because they will never come again. We are, after all, only mortal."

Riker managed a smile. "Speak for yourself, sir. I kinda planned on living forever."

The first officer bent down and picked up the captain's chair. He tried to set it upright where it had once stood so proudly, but it was no good. It was broken.

He muttered, "I always thought I'd have a crack at this chair one day."

The captain put his hand on the commander's

shoulder. "You may still. Somehow I doubt if this will be the last ship to carry the name *Enterprise.*"

He touched his comm badge. "Picard to *Farragut.* Two to beam up."

In two swirling columns of light, Picard and Riker vanished from the planet of Veridian Three.

About the Author

JOHN VORNHOLT was born in Marion, Ohio, and knew he wanted to write science fiction when he discovered Doc Savage novels and the words of Edgar Rice Burroughs. But somehow he wrote nonfiction and television scripts for many years, including animated series such as *Dennis the Menace, Ghostbusters,* and *Super Mario Brothers.* He was also an actor and playwright, with several published plays to his credit.

John didn't get back to his first love—writing SF—until 1989 with the publication of his first Star Trek Next Generation novel, *Masks.* He wrote two more, *Contamination* and *War Drums;* a classic Trek novel, *Sanctuary;* and a Deep Space Nine novel, *Antimatter.* For young readers, he's also written *Starfleet Academy #4: Capture the Flag.* All of these titles are available from Pocket Books.

John is also the author of several nonfiction books for kids and the novel *How to Sneak into the Girls' Locker Room.*

John lives in Tucson, Arizona, with his wife, Nancy, his children, Sarah and Eric, and his dog, Bessie.

Beam aboard for new adventures!

A new title every other month!

Pocket Books presents a new, illustrated series for younger readers based on the hit television show STAR TREK: DEEP SPACE NINE®.

Young Jake Sisko is looking for friends aboard the space station. He finds Nog, a Ferengi his own age, and together they find a whole lot of trouble!

#1: THE STAR GHOST
#2: STOWAWAYS
by Brad Strickland

#3: PRISONERS OF PEACE
by John Peel

#4: THE PET
by Mel Gilden and Ted Pedersen

Published by Pocket Books

954-03